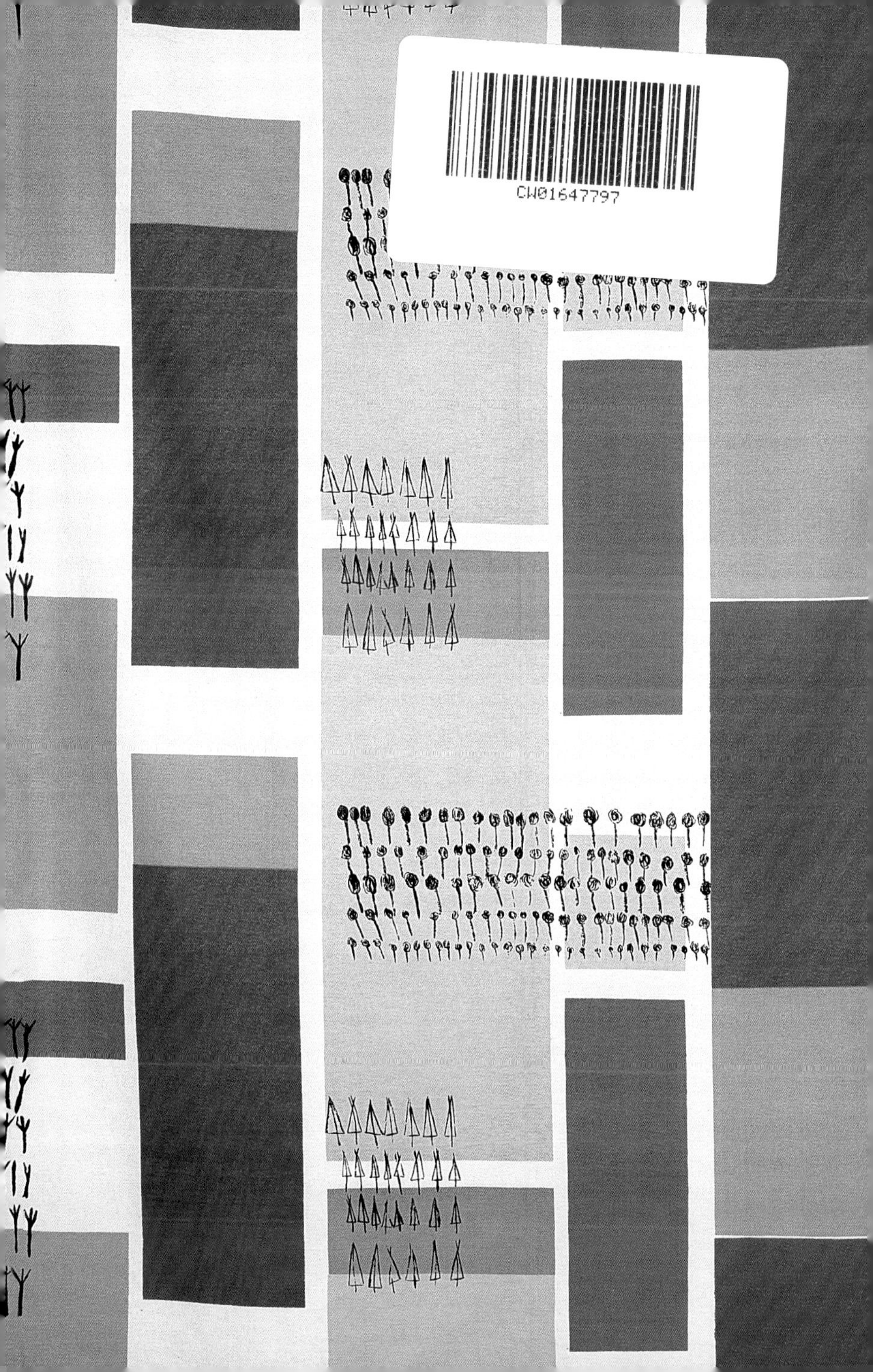

LETTICE DELMER

Persephone Book Nº 36
Published by Persephone Books Ltd 2002

First published 1958 by The Linden Press

Endpapers taken from 'Plantation', a 1958 screen-printed
cotton crepe designed by Lucienne Day for Heal's

Typeset in ITC Baskerville by Keystroke,
Jacaranda Lodge, Wolverhampton

Colour by Cheney & Sons Ltd, Banbury

Printed and bound by Biddles Ltd,
Guildford and King's Lynn

ISBN 1 903155 215

Persephone Books Ltd
59 Lamb's Conduit Street
London WC1N 3NB
020 7242 9292

www.persephonebooks.co.uk

LETTICE DELMER

by

SUSAN MILES

PERSEPHONE BOOKS
LONDON

PUBLISHER'S NOTE

****

A couple of years ago a Persephone reader wrote to tell us about a 1958 book by his mother; enclosed with his letter was a photocopy of its jacket. We duly went off to the British Library and looked at it and alas decided it was not for us; but noticed that on the back of the jacket a novel in verse was announced with a 'puff' by TS Eliot.

Lettice Delmer (beautiful title) turned out to have that unputdownable quality that is, we hope, the hallmark of a Persephone book. It was also in an unusual genre that began with wandering minstrels round the fire, continued with Chaucer and *Don Juan, Eugene Onegin* and *Aurora Leigh* and recently culminated in Vikram Seth's *The Golden Gate* (1986) – a novel, ie a narrative with plot, characterisation and psychological insight, where the verse form is readable, not too intrusive – but essential.

'Susan Miles' was the *nom de plume* of Ursula Roberts, this much we could discover. But it has been difficult to find out very much more about her. There is, however, *Portrait of a Parson*, the small biography she wrote of her husband, an outstandingly intelligent and compassionate clergyman named William Roberts (1873–1953). From this we learn that he

****

married the then Ursula Wyllie when he was thirty-five and she was twenty-one, and was Rector at Crick in Northamptonshire from 1909–17 (apart from six months teaching in Delhi). The causes closest to both their hearts were socialism, pacifism and feminism, and his outspoken views on women's suffrage and the ordination of women probably hindered his career. Ursula Roberts once said as much to Maude Royden, the famous suffragette and a friend; and one can imagine the Bishop's reaction when William wrote letters to the papers denouncing forcible feeding or took a horse from its shafts 'and patiently perambulated the village streeets, leading him, festooned with the colours of the National Union of Women's Suffrage Societies.'

The Roberts, who had no children of their own, were deeply hospitable and the Rectory became a haven for the homeless, the needy and the unlucky. 'There were those who stayed for months, even for years . . . Friends and relatives came freely, little nieces staying for weeks together.' This limitless generosity continued when, in 1917, they went to the beautiful Hawksmoor church, St George's in Hart Street (now New Oxford Street) Bloomsbury, a living that had become vacant after the death of the Rev. Baumgarten, a fellow stalwart of the Church League for Women's Suffrage.

Here, for more than twenty years, they were a centre of the Anglican community in London, watching with broad-minded compassion over an enormously varied congregation. This included the beneficiaries of such organisations as the Society for Virtuous Spinsters and the Assocation for Moral and Social

****

Hygiene as well as a large community of doctors, civil servants, teachers and other professionals; they were friends with Dick Sheppard, Vicar of St Martin-in-the-Fields, pioneer of religious broadcasting and a leading pacifist of the '30s; 'TS Eliot, JC Squire, LS Stebbing, Laurence Binyon, Middleton Murry, Helen Waddell, Harold Munro and Herbert Palmer – some of whom were parishioners – were among those who were glad to give their services as lecturers' wrote Susan Miles in the biography of her husband. All were friends, which is why Susan Stebbing, Storm Jameson and Katherine Mansfield were among the dedicatees of her books.

Of the circumstances surrounding her life as a writer little is known. She began by publishing poetry in periodicals ranging from suffragette newspapers to the *New Statesman*. *Dunch*, her first volume of poetry, appeared in 1918 and contains one or two poems which would have shocked the parish should they have read them, for example 'A Reaction', which begins:

> I do not want to discuss the price of flannelette with the
> doctor's wife
> I do not care whether flannelette costs fivepence three
> farthings
> Or fivepence halfpenny.
> I do not want to decide how many loaves of bread for
> the school treat
> Shall be white
> And how many shall be Standard. . .

and goes on

> I do not want to visit the churchwarden's wife
> She will use her saw-like voice on me and will deplore
> the fact
> That I 'don't visit'.
> She will tell me that I should make 'quite a nice little
> parson's wife',
> If only I would give up all that silly nonsense about the
> Vote
> And turn my thoughts to duties
> That lie near home.

Three more small volumes of poetry appeared in the years from 1922–4. She published one novel in 1934 and another in 1942. Finally *Lettice Delmer* was published in 1958. However, it received little attention, being in an unfashionable form and on an unfashionable theme.

But recently Susan Miles was mentioned in *The Observer*. The late Ian Hamilton thought of trying to update Samuel Johnson's *Lives of the Poets*, and discovered that he had only heard of ten of them; some were listed in Margaret Drabble's *Oxford Companion to English Literature* simply because they had appeared in Johnson's *Lives*. 'Not even Johnson's hospitality had been sufficient to protect them from the final darkness.'

Hamilton decided to make his own list of fifty poets whom he would include in a twentieth-century *Lives* and turned first to Harold Monro's 1920 list of fifty *Contemporary Poets;* Susan Miles was mentioned in a chapter about a group of eleven that

****

includes Ford Madox Ford and Ezra Pound. He turned then to Michael Roberts's *Faber Book of Modern Verse* (1935): very few poets are on both lists – only Lawrence, the Sitwells, Ezra Pound, Graves, Herbert Read and HD. Many had vanished in fifteen years; Susan Miles was one.

What is sobering is that someone who was singled out as one of the fifty foremost post-First World War poets could vanish so utterly. One of her poems, 'The Cenotaph', appeared in a Virago anthology of First World War poetry by women and its tone is immediately arresting in its irony and lack of pomposity. But apparently no PHD student or poetry lover ever went in search of its author.

Because we know so little about Susan Miles we do not even know whether *Lettice Delmer*, which spans the years of the First World War and the 1920s, was written at the time it was set or in the 1950s. One's instinct is for the former, but it could easily have been written between 1955 (when she published the biography of her husband) and 1957, especially with the 'room of one's own' ie time to herself allowed to a widow. Indeed, she did publish a small volume of poetry in 1962 *(A Morsel of Gold)* in which one or two of the poems have the tone of *Lettice Delmer*; on the other hand these too could have been in a bottom drawer since the 1920s and there are small clues that lead to this interpretation, for example there is a poem about two young women called Beattie and Mab (Beatrice and Mabel), names that were far more popular before the Second World War than after.

Clearly *Lettice Delmer* has some elements arising out of Susan Miles's own life. The novel begins during the First World War,

****

with Mrs Delmer visiting a 'Special Hospital' in her capacity as wife of the doctor attached to the hospital. The Rev. Roberts, as newly-installed Rector of St George's, Bloomsbury, had, in 1917, taken on 'the Chaplaincy of a London County Council Hospital for women and girls with venereal disease' (*Portrait of a Parson*). This was almost certainly the London Lock Hospital in the Harrow Road, Paddington, the word lock deriving either from 'locking up', or from the Old French 'loques' meaning rags or dressings applied to the sores of lepers. By the early twentieth century the Paddington Lock Hospital was for women suffering from venereal disease and for unmarried mothers; by 1918, when a competition was announced for improving the hospital and designing a new building, it was more than ever in need of the voluntary help that Mrs Roberts and, in the novel, Mrs Delmer, were eager to give.

The Delmers decide to invite an inmate of the Special Hospital to live with them in their home in Highgate, and to allow her to bring her little boy of five who has been living in an orphanage. Her name is Flora Tort (flower wronged), one of those whom the real-life William Roberts saw as 'the pathetic victim of other people's lusts', believing humbly that 'all sinners were fellow-sinners' (p.65 *Portrait of a Parson*); the description of this episode must have been based on Ursula Roberts's experiences as wife of an ever-hospitable rector. But the Roberts were unconventional enough to understand their own motives – that there is no such thing as pure altruism. The experiment the Delmers put in train is a failure because, as Flora Tort understands, '"You didn't want me. You never liked me. It was all for Christ . . . I hate you. *Hate* you.'"

****

The victim is eighteen year-old Lettice, the pampered daughter of the house who, as so often at that time, has been given nothing to do with her life except wait for marriage, who is innocent, egocentric and bored, takes refuge in daydreams, and is not even interested in the progress of the war because: 'I can't enter into it: pin flags/study the papers and the maps each day.' Pages 50–60 contain an unusually perceptive and understanding portrait of a young girl who is arrogant, unformed and uncertain yet arouses all one's sympathies because it is so easy to see what has gone wrong for her. When she discovers, in the cottage in Gospel Oak, that the Highgate neighbour, whom she had considered 'hers', is in love with their maid, her bruised pride and rage is painfully articulated. Her 'devilish' attitude is something she will pay for all her life and although her friends and family try to help her, Susan Miles allows her heroine no respite until she has found complete humility. The clue is in her name: lettice/delmer means happy one/out of the sea, or deep; by the end it is she who has found salvation and been redeemed. (As Dick Sheppard wrote to Laurence Housman in 1930: 'Christianity is the only religion that has faced the problem of suffering and dared to believe that out of darkness there will one day come light.')

Which elements in *Lettice Delmer* are taken from Susan Miles's life we may never know. Clearly some things are autobiographical, for example we know that the young Ursula Wyllie went to school in Highgate, so it is possible that her family lived in Fitzroy Park like the Delmers. Lettice writes poetry: 'Soon I ought to hear/if Elkin Mathews means to take

****

the book' she says to her brother, Elkin Mathews being the publisher of Susan Miles's third volume of poetry, *The Hares* (1924). Later, full of grief and remorse, she says: 'I've *played* at art and music./ And Blackwell's right: those sonnets *are* derived,/ and more than *somewhat* stilted.' Blackwell was Susan Miles's publisher for her first two books; could they then have rejected *The Hares* as being derivative and stilted?

If the book does have personal elements Susan Miles may have written it in secret and chosen not to publish until after her husband's death. Another factor may have been that it could be read as an implied criticism of one of her husband's greatest and most celebrated virtues, celebrated at his Memorial Service, when thanks were given 'for his compassion for the despised, the suffering and the exiled, and for his willingness to welcome them into his home.' Then again, Susan Miles might not have wanted to reveal her possible ambivalence about her home being open to all comers, honest or dishonest. Finally, some aspects of the novel might simply have been deemed too shocking to publish earlier.

The sentences that originally caught our attention on the jacket flap were: 'I find it a very poignant story' (TS Eliot); 'Its simplicities are at a profound level. The theme is a great one and the characters superb'(Storm Jameson); and 'I am impressed by the originality and utter genuineness of this novel in verse. It is a form which has gone far too long untried' (Rayner Heppenstall). They are judgements that we would endorse even more now that our first, hurried reading in the British Library has turned into the leisurely re-readings that we hope will be enjoyed by Persephone readers.

LIST OF CHARACTERS

Mrs Delmer
Lettice Delmer, her daughter aged eighteen
Hulbert Delmer, Lettice's half-brother and Mrs Delmer's stepson, a medical research student
Dr Rendell Delmer, Lettice and Hulbert's father, and retiring Harley Street doctor
Flora Tort, patient at the Special Hospital
Derrick Tort, her son, aged five
Helen Cordell, a Special Hospital visitor
Francis Conway, friend of Hulbert Delmer
Annie, the Delmers' maid
Mrs Bonner, former maid to the Delmers, who now does the laundry
Cherry Bonner, her daughter
Miss Hobley, hostel-worker
Bois Diego, a fellow Harrovian of Hulbert's
Miss Flint, landlady at Pyrte
Hugh Fennemore, paying guest of Miss Flint's
Mr Briggs, Flora Tort's husband
Delmer Conway, Cherry's first child
Irene, Lettice's friend
Joan, Irene's daughter
Richard Fennemore, Hugh's father, Rector of Bittersby

There is a summary of the plot of *Lettice Delmer* at the end of this volume, should the story need clarification.

LETTICE DELMER

****

Lettice Delmer

Blatant clangs the bell,
crude as the diseases that gaol the patients
in the Special Hospital.
However gently Mrs. Delmer pulls,
the noise, although anticipated,
startles and horrifies her.
Tremulous and cowering,
every other Thursday Mrs. Delmer waits,
flayed by the fear that each unheeding passer
thinks her a patient seeking shamed admission
—or the mother of a patient.
The porter dislikes visitors,
especially on a day that is not a visiting day.
He is pushing some trolley laden with soiled dressings,
or stoking some furnace in some remote cellar,
glad to humiliate
the white-haired, young-faced, delicately flushing
    fine lady,
who, in his view, doctor's wife or no doctor's wife,
has no business to have truck with Special patients.
Mrs. Delmer's hand in its membrane-tenuous
    pale glove
checks,

and withdraws from a second pulling at the hated
bell-chain.
It lifts one light corner of a cloth that covers a rush
basket.
Mrs. Delmer shrinks away from thinking of the
porter,
or the passers, or the barred and coarsened patients.
She stoops and with tremulous lips
brushes the petals of a primula,
seeking courage.
Her thoughts frame facile verse.

Lovely dainty flowers,
gathered in dawn's dew,
virginal and fragrant,
let me live in you.

Let me sense the sweetness
from those gentle hands
that, intent on service,
laid you in your bands,

bound you into posies,
fresh and exquisite:
cowslip, hyacinth, daphne,
primrose, violet;

tied you with pale ribbons
—that once decked soft hair—
damped by young dew-wet fingers,
smoothed with punctilious care.

Lettice, lovely daughter,
Lettice, wholesome, nesh,
breathe on me your fragrance,
Lettice, flower-fresh,

innocent and tender
  as this primrose bud,
Lettice, stepping sweetly
  into womanhood!

The porter has bulled his snorting way across
  the yard.
Creaking at the joints, he labours the heavy bolts
and grudgingly gives entrance.
Mrs. Delmer follows him,
past the trolley laden with metal containers of
  loathsome burnables,
up harsh cold steps,
along harsh cold corridors,
to the door of Matron's office,
marked *Private: knock and wait*.
The porter knocks and waits,
giving at intervals his bull-like snort.
Ugly presage,
hateful presage,
in all that Mrs. Delmer shrinkingly senses.
Patients shuffle by from treatment.
Some as they pass the porter mouth a greeting
or a curse,
answered by never a word
though sometimes by a wink.
The painted walls, bile-green with ox-blood dado,
scabbed and peeled above the hot-water pipes,
seem to Mrs. Delmer to be closing in on her.
A catch, released by Matron, opens the door at last
with sinister slowness.
Mrs. Delmer is accepted in silence

with a curt nod that bids her sit
and wait.

'All wrong, all wrong, if Matron put me first;
ward-maid and wife of world-famed specialist,
equal in God's sight should be so in hers,
His handmaid.'
Though she has prayed successfully for grace,
she sighs; but soon, making an effort, smiles.
The reprimanded ward-maid shuffles out;
the smile's unheeded.
Matron consults her memorandum-pad,
then briefly emits orders, clipped, precise.
"Bald girl in Single Ward—it's her own fault.
Don't show her any sympathy. She threw
her antidote to arsenic down the drain.
And, Mrs. Delmer, this is serious:
I told you the first time you visited
never to shake a patient by the hand.
A Sister saw you shake a patient's hand
on your last visit."
The tender pink of Mrs. Delmer's cheeks
has turned deep rose. "The girl held out her hand.
I'm sorry . . ." The embarrassed voice trails dumb.
('Ah, how convey to hygiened competence
Christ's *Inasmuch* compelling shrinking flesh. . .?')
"Well, see it doesn't happen any more,
or else these unofficial visits cease.
I'm not at all convinced they're beneficial."
'Oh, nor am I!' cries Mrs. Delmer's heart.
Suddenly Matron smiles.
"What have you there? More sweets? You spoil
those gals.

—No! I can smell. It's cowslips. Oooh, and
    daphne!"
Shy Mrs. Delmer has drawn back the cloth,
pleased to be smiled at.
"My daughter made the posies: *her* idea."
"Oh, pretty! Pretty! Let me sniff again.
Why, bless me, what a life your gal must lead
that she has time to fidget with such fallals!"
Matron is sunk in hospital accounts
before the door has closed on Delmer's wife,
who tiptoes past 'Maternity', to pause
outside the ward where pity must not knock.
Quite bald? A *young* girl? Show no sympathy?
Does not the stipulation set her free
from the ordeal?
Show, Matron said; she didn't say express.
How could one not *show* pity? She has turned;
she stands in hesitation, breathing fast.
'Evasion!—Courage: knock.' She enters, shrinking.
A turnip head, gashed by a gap-toothed slit,
dismays and startles.
Grim lashless eyes, large pupilled,
view listlessly the proffered primroses.
"I haven't got no vause. Put 'em down there."
Baulked, Mrs. Delmer finds no utterance.
Unspoken musings shape themselves, unwilled,
while Turnip-head feigns sleep.

Lovely dainty flowers,
  gathered in dawn's dew,
virginal and fragrant,
  there's no vause for you.

Pitchpine table, centred
  with a shiny round,
stencilled with puce roses
  on an acid ground,

matching walls and dado
  in their noisome hues. . .
Offered here or Hades,
  which would Lettice choose?

Desperate, she disciplines her thoughts and cries:
"It's such a lovely day! Almost like June!"
"Not in this bloody hole, stuck here in bed.
Don't see no sky nor sunshine, only wall."
'No pity. No compassion. . .
Oh, why did I bring posies? Why not sweets?
Why not *Home Chats* that wouldn't need a vause?
Oh, dreadful place, where posies have no place,
nor pity, place!'
Curbed from heart's utterance, feebly she rebukes,
knowing her utterance feeble, hating it.
"You shouldn't use that word." She turns and flees,
seeing the lightning flash in lashless eyes
and sensing that the thunder will roll loud.
She steals a moment in the corridor
to pray herself courageous,
then (with a thumping heart and trembling knees)
pushes the heavy door of the day-ward.

The room has a north aspect,
north by east.
The girls wear scanty clothing,
facilitating treatment.

North aspect, lowered vitality, bare legs,
necessitate central heating,
even in June-warm April.
The girls sit face to wall,
feet on the water-pipes.
Several are far advanced in pregnancy.
One is piloted by a stolid nurse
towards the Labour Ward.
The others stare.
A group plays cribbage,
the cards soiled and dog-eared.
One or two heads turn
to gape at Mrs. Delmer.
No word comes
or nod in sign of welcome.

Only as Thy servant
  dare I stay, dear Lord:
only in Thy service,
  only at Thy word.

Every native fibre
  every native shred,
bids me to flee encounter,
  dumb and discomfited.

Thin shod and from behind them,
  in stealth I seem to creep,
impertinent, intrusive,
  as wolf among the sheep:

Thy sheep, Thy lambs, good Shepherd,
  these who have lost their way.
Let Thy love be my staff, Lord!
  Use me—as shepherd-boy.

The shepherd-boy steps forward, would-be brave,
but shrinking still in spirit.
The weather is a topic fraught with risk,
and any less impersonal approach
—a question as to crochet—may evoke
a 'Nosey Parker', snuffled in retort.
One topic, and one only, may provide
a basis for exchange unfraught by risk.
To a new-comer Mrs. Delmer's voice
tosses the same shy word-bait on each visit.
Had not the lashless stare of Turnip-head
startled the fish-hook from her,
perhaps in place of scutter might have chanced
a bite
to shepherd-boy-cum-fisher.
Choosing for catch a broad and comely back,
erect and stalwart, under a white nape
and burnished hair coiled neatly,
she swings her line and, as it swirls, there turns
a face, shrewd, handsome, hard, alert, and bold.
"Perhaps you know my husband, Dr. Delmer?"
Almost the hard face softens.
"You're Mrs. *Delmer*, Madam? *Please* sit down."
While Mrs. Delmer meekly nips the bud
of smug approval swelling in her breast
to hear the 'Madam',
the well-trained parlourmaid stands by the
chair
vacated when she rose, and points to it.
'This *is* the girl that Rendell spoke about;
I'm sure it must be she. So trim, polite
and so superior in speech,' reflects

shy Mrs. Delmer.
"Kindness itself," the girl is murmuring.
"Madam, perhaps. . ." (she coughs and droops
her lids)
"he may have mentioned my predicament?"
"He told me something. . .
He didn't mention any name, of course."
"Oh, but why not? My name is Flora Tort.
I hope I know my manners and my place;
and anyway I know a gentleman. . .
Courteous he's always been, for all I've got
in this disgraceful scrape through my own fault:
though not the only one to blame,
that's obvious, Madam."
Embarrassment makes Mrs. Delmer's tongue
slide into speech it frightens her to hear.
"My husband said you wondered . . . you would
like
to trace your little boy . . . to make your home
in service with some kindly family . . .
It crossed my mind—"
(She pauses while she does not say aloud
'only to be dismissed as soon as thought')
"that possibly *we* might have made a home
for him and you."
"But, Madam, that would be too wonderful!
To wait on Dr. Delmer!
But why build flimsy castles in the air?
I'd never trace the child after so long."
('And do I really want to?' Flora thinks.)
She ponders how to extricate herself,
while Mrs. Delmer wings a flustered prayer.

O God, forgive!
  I was about to pray
  (Oh piteous waif and stray!)
let him not live, not live!
  Or let her never trace
  (Ah base! Ah base!)
the son she bore in lonely agony!
O God, forgive!
  In penitence I pray
  now that she *may*
trace the child blessedly,
  and, God, I vow
  that—Rendell wishing it—
I will ensconce this woman in our house
in place of Annie, should she marry soon.
  Even I pray
that Annie soon *shall* marry and be gone.
Only Thy grace can give me strength for this!
  Give me Thy grace, Thy grace!

With such intensity she prays for grace
that, without knowing, she has clasped her hands,
relaxing hold on the rush basket poised
precariously on her too sloping lap.
Lettice's flowers lie among plimsolled feet,
hot from their contact with the water-pipes
and smelling of warm rubber and themselves.
Flora Tort stoops,
more as a housemaid trained to tidy ways
than in distress at spring's frail loveliness
debased to lie in squalor.
"Thank you! Oh, thank you! They've begun to wilt
in this hot room; they're bruised, too, by their fall;
and nobody will have a pot or jug. . ."
The thought of all the care

Lettice has lavished on the wasted gifts
grieves Mrs. Delmer.
She takes her timid leave of Flora Tort.
Giftless, she lacks all courage to pursue
the wonted circuit of the dismal wards.
The porter, summoned from his squalid tasks
to turn the grating key and let her out,
snorts his bull-snort and curls a cynic lip,
slamming the gates behind her.

Bruised and wilting petals,
  once so fresh and gay,
gathered by soft fingers
  at the break of day:

thrust them now with refuse
  in the litter-rack
clamped against the railing
  of the rusty park.

Leave them on a huddle
  of banana skins,
orange peel, old papers,
  tea leaves, sardine tins.

Nevermore shall treasure
  blessed by Letty's touch
cross that sin-smirched threshold,
  know corruption's smutch.

Leave them, leave them, leave them!
  Home—to Letty now!
Hail a passing hansom;
  forget the sin, the woe:

Turnip-head and Flora,
  Flora's abandoned boy.
Home, home, to love, to Letty!
  To innocence and joy!

The bell clangs again, harsh and loud.
Someone is watching Mrs. Delmer:
someone who stands
where an hour ago Mrs. Delmer stood.
Mrs. Delmer notes the waiting figure.
Helen Cordell's features are irregular,
the nose slightly crooked,
the eyes deep-set and slanting,
the large mouth mobile.
There is zest in her and vividness;
there is that which Mrs. Delmer sums up as
'character'.
Corn-flower blue eyes,
symmetrical features,
fine white hair,
delicate skin without a wrinkle,
seem to their owner, suddenly, insipid.
'A lady, undoubtedly a lady;
yet she is waiting—'
Mrs. Delmer flushes in shame to find in herself
the curiosity she resentfully attributed an hour ago
to others.
She hurries on,
but at the corner of the street
her head swivels, unbidden,
and at what she sees she checks her steps,
astonished.

How *could* she? How *could* she?
Pilfered from garbage-bin,
smirched by banana skin,
orange peel, sardine tin. . .
How *could* she? How *could* she?

Mrs. Delmer hurries towards hansom cab and home,
turning no more to look at Helen Cordell,
who, heedless of passers-by,
darts back across the road
just as the porter draws his grating bolts
to give her entrance.
Tucking Lettice Delmer's posy into her belt,
Helen Cordell follows the snorting porter with
springing gait,
insouciant and erect.

* * * *

Tap of the hansom horse's plodding hooves
dictates the rhythm of the thoughts that jog
between the shafts of Mrs. Delmer's brain,
as in her hackney vehicle she homes,
dismissing all that puzzles or disgusts
or horrifies her.

Annie will have a bath prepared
and fresh clothes pure as Aaron's.
Not till I've bathed shall Letty twine
her tendril fingers round me.
Water, its perfume barely sensed,
shall purge each pore to fragrance,
and every hair, fine-kempt, shall prove
its innocence and freshness.
What can I say if Letty asks
about her dainty posies?
—Why, tell how Matron sniffed their scent,
and cried: "Oh, pretty! Pretty!"
and then, quick, turn the talk aside
to Letty, Letty, Letty. . .

When Fitzroy Park is reached, so well content
is Letty's mother to be home again
that she is lavish both with smiles and tip.
Blessings go with her as her little feet
trip up the front-door steps of Number Three
to the wide porch that welcomes.
Almost before the bell's vibrations cease
the door comes open on its well-oiled hinge
and Annie beams her greeting.
"Oh, Ma'm, you've come. . ." ('She looks so tired
    and pale,
have I the heart to tell my happy tale?')
The blushing maid abashed and silent stands,
pleating her apron in her trembling hands.
"He's spoken, Annie?" "Ma'm he's had a rise.
He wants it to be soon, Ma'm." "Such bright eyes!
I see how glad he's made you. Oh, I prayed
that he would ask you, Annie!" "—Ma'am, you
    prayed?
But you don't *want* to lose me?" "No, no, no.
I can't explain. But, Annie, it was so."
'Dear God control my coward fears.
Choke back the weakness of these coward tears.
If Flora comes, she comes as sent by Thee:
my penance to receive her, it may be.'
"My bath is ready, Annie?"
('What if some caller came and found us pat
kissing and crying on the front-door mat?')
"The water's hot, the towels are warm,
clean linen aired and spread;
the pearl and oyster *crêpe-de-chine*
is waiting on the bed."

While Mrs. Delmer bathes she hears the thud
of tennis-balls, and hearing it is glad
to know that Hulbert has put up the net
and fetched his friend and neighbour for a game
with darling Lettice. Words, she does not hear
but she can trace her daughter's treble notes,
her step-son's bass, and Francis Conway's tenor,
as score and comments rise and fall and check
beyond the ha-ha and the flower-beds.
She leaves the bathroom and withdraws to don
her *crêpe-de-chine*,
pleased by the thought that Lettice will be pleased
to see that she has had it aired and pressed
after its hibernation.
The balls still thud when each fine loop is hooked
and Annie's patient fingers are set free
to fetch the tea-tray.
"Fault. Double fault. Game: set," scores the
    bass voice.
"Oh sorry, partner," murmurs the shamed tenor.
"You're out of practice, Francis.
The first play of the season, and old balls. . ."
Gracious and bland the treble voice consoles.
"The same for you and Hulbert. . . " "Play again?"
Hulbert scoops up a ball, and waits detached.
"Mama will soon be coming. I'll drop out—
Why, here she comes!" cries Lettice.
She trips across the lawn with arms outstretched.
Her mother cries "My darling!" They embrace.
Francis is greeted warmly. Tea is poured.
Unsmiling, Hulbert waits
(punctiliously courteous, but aloof)

on his step-mother, half-sister, and friend.
"The voyage was a good one, Francis dear?"
"Oh, not bad, Mrs. Delmer, on the whole:
but six weeks leave! In sunshine!" "It won't last."
Hulbert's deep voice breaks in impatiently.
"April's not June: admitted. But I've hopes."
Smiling and placid, Mrs. Delmer sips,
feasting her eyes on Lettice, snowdrop-pure
in her cool dress with pale jade ornament.

'Lettice, stepping sweetly
  into womanhood. . .
Someday, sweet Lettice Conway?
  Romping in merry mood

with boys, as sound as Francis,
  girls, gay as she is gay,
pure as a dawn, lark-carolled,
  in an unclouded May?'

When tea is finished daydreams linger still.
Mother and daughter, hand in hand, relaxed,
stay, chatting fondly, in their cushioned chairs.
They watch the men, eyes following the ball.
The feelings Hulbert copes with do not break
into the tranquil pool of their content.
They view his motions as an active male's,
intent on winning,
not as the symptoms of a soul disturbed,
who smites a foe garbed as a tennis-ball,
making a weapon of his tennis bat.

Francis is playing better now that Lettice rests.
He deferred too much to her,

fearful lest he should poach,
fearful lest he should fail her.
Hulbert's fierce downstrokes test him.
He responds with swift back-handers.
He is aware of Hulbert's mood:
of his fierce antipathy to his step-mother's docile
compliance with his father's wishes.
No snorting porter pushing burnables could feel
half so strongly as does Hulbert
the incongruity,
the outrage,
of the task imposed.
Francis is aware that Hulbert's passionate distaste
finds a relief
in smashing at the ball,
which, for the moment, is his father's will.
Francis has loved Hulbert since they wore sailor-
suits and played with catapults.
His love is profound and chaste and delicately
intuitive.
Now he serves his friend with faultless service
deliberately aimed to draw its meet response.
Hulbert calls no score;
only when ladies play are tongues kept wagging to
hold diffused attention.
Each taut male holds deuce between his teeth,
unvocal.
Two points to Hulbert's demon;
then game and set, and exeunt (donning sweaters)
the bonded males.

April is June no longer. Lettice loops
her mother's cloak about her. "*Pretty* dress!
The tiny tucks, the little silver moons!
Silver and pearl and oyster: just the shades
to make a setting for your lovely skin."
"It barely hooks. I'm getting far too plump."
"No, not one bit! Plumpness is right—in you.
Oh, are you *very* tired?
You really shouldn't use that cable-tram:
it's far too jolty." "I came home by cab:
a hansom, Letty." "Well, I'm glad of that.
But I'm quite sure the brougham would be best.
Why won't you use the brougham when you go
to visit Daddy's patients?"
But Mrs. Delmer turns the probe aside.
She cannot say: Because of the cold glint
that I should see in Fuller's eye, the flick
that I should sense from Fuller's swirling lash,
to hear my destination. . . So instead
she folds her cloak more closely as she gives
a little evening shiver after warmth
and bids her daughter hurry in to change.
Annie comes out to meet them. "Master's here!
—He's early, Ma'm, but there is nothing wrong!"
she adds to ease the quick anxiety
she sees flit through her mistress at the news.
"And how did my brave envoy fare today?"
asks Rendell Delmer in his dressing-room
as Lois Delmer joins him for the chat
that is for both habitual as a meal
and as sustaining.
"How have *you* fared? You didn't have to wait

to get your breath today? No horrid pills?"
"Only two! Nursemaid-Fuller seized my bag
and saw I didn't hurry.
He's my solicitous shadow since that faint."
"That's such a comfort to me!—But two pills. . .
I wish you didn't need the things at all."
"Little fusspot!—Now *your* adventures, please!"
"Oh, you'll be disappointed—but glad, too.
I only spoke to two girls. One was rude,
the other most polite: the one you spoke of."
Partly in dread, but partly, too, in pride,
she lets the rest rush from her breathlessly.
Her husband turns, a hair-brush in each hand,
and in his eyes pride and astonishment,
and twinkling mirth.
"What about Annie? Martha wouldn't mind,
but Annie, bless her. . !" "Well, I knew of course
it couldn't happen unless Annie left.
You know I told you how I'd come to think
the baker's roundsman was in love with her
and might propose soon? Well—I prayed he would!
And when I saw her, saw her shining eyes,
I knew he *had*."
"But do you *want* Annie to go away
and Flora Tort to come? You say you—*prayed*?"
"I prayed in penitence,
because I'd nearly prayed that you would fail
to trace the little boy—"
A sudden shout of laughter interrupts,
checked on the instant.
In Rendell's arms she sighs, drawn here, drawn there,
by contrary emotions: pride to know

Rendell's approval of her, dread of change
from Annie's homely service
(kind and familiar as old corsets, eased
by wont and wearing)
to Flora Tort's—constricting, menacing.
Embarrassment that shirks a hateful theme
troubles her utterance to a tone so hushed
Rendell can barely hear it.
"There couldn't be a risk. . ? You're really sure?
A risk to darling Letty?"
"No, no, indeed not! Six weeks more at most
and Flora'll be as sound as she." A sigh. . .
For Rendell his wife's sigh breathes pure relief,
but actually there is in it regret
since even the faintest risk would have expunged
all duty to materialise the plan.
And now the second gong drowns sighs and speech,
bidding all problems wait till dinner's done.
Loving as Annie and her baker-man,
the Delmers go to dinner, fingers twined.

* * * *

Rendell's assurance has been justified.
Dressed in a neat costume, Flora Tort sits,
beside her anxious mistress-soon-to-be,
waiting reunion with her little son.
Few and impoverished the regulars
who share the vigil. Sunk in apathy,
these wait and gape in undernourished sloth.
On sagging laps mouth-breathing infants drool,
layered in flannelette and dingy wool

felted by helpless washing. Flora Tort
eyes them with cold disfavour. "It's as well
that there will be an opportunity
to do some shopping with the little boy
before we come to live in Fitzroy Park.
I'll fetch him with a cab
and take him straight to Gorringe's, or Glave's,
tomorrow morning. I should be ashamed
to have him in a bus in workhouse duds."
A loud sneeze breaks the thread of Flora's thoughts.
She blows her nose with a vast trumpeting.
"The draught is something chronic.
No waterpipes. . . My feet are like two stones.
I wish they'd hurry up and bring the child."
"It must be *such* a strain. . ."
Wrenched by compassion Mrs. Delmer broods,
unable to express all that she feels.
'How could I have *lived*
if *Lettice* had been lost for five long years. . .'
There comes a sudden thought: 'Has Flora nothing?
Perhaps she too has a balloon unblown,
tucked in her handbag?' Diffident and shy,
she seeks to ease the tension—drawing out
from her own reticule her daughter's gifts.
"Miss Lettice painted this for you to show.
Here is the dormer window of your room;
and his is next it. (There's a door between.)
She sent these chocolates too, and the balloon..
Perhaps *you* have one waiting to be blown?
(Little boys love them, don't they?) And if so,
this one need not be given. . ." "I can find
a sixpence for the child. I never thought

to bring him playthings."
"You give the chocolates: wouldn't that be best?"
"You give him what you've brought him, Madam,
thanks."
Flora is huffed, and Mrs. Delmer—snubbed—
flushing, takes up the wrinkled limp balloon.
Roused from her apathy a mother pokes
her listless infant. "See the lady, duck."
But Mrs. Delmer, scarlet and confused,
has no more breath or courage. Both collapse:
balloon and blower.
The listless infant drowses once again,
while Mrs. Delmer prays, then purses lips,
blows with renewed resolve,
and this time triumphs. Fumbling with the string,
she looks appealingly at Flora Tort,
whose competent quick fingers pull it tight
and knot it neatly:
responsive to a call for dextrous touch,
not in compassion. Suddenly the door
swings open and a strident voice blares out:
"Is anybody here for the child Tort?"
Cowering beside the woman, Derrick stands,
cropped like a convict, scrubbed, and grimly draped
in a black pinafore a size too big,
from which his sticks of legs grotesquely slope
in woollen stockings, darned and darned again:
a knock-kneed scarecrow.
—Here's Mrs. Delmer half across the room
before she knows she's risen from the bench.
The scarlet globe swings bravely at her wrist.
Derrick, his action unwilled as her own,

takes a step forward. Not on her balloon
his gaze is fastened, but on her sweet face.
Her tender eyes,
meeting his eyes, are liars for a flash.
But now she catches breath, takes a step back,
and points at Flora Tort. "Your mother, Derrick."
Without another glance toward the child,
blindly she stares into the gravelled yard,
at stunted bushes, rusty iron rails,
a peeling plane tree. She shuts to her mind,
refusing entrance to a mother's words
at such a meeting with her sundered child.
Almost before a faltering phrase has formed
within her tremulous mind her prayer's cut short.
"I think he wonders whose is the balloon.
He keeps on staring."
"It is for you, dear Derrick. Take the string."
Balloons and kisses equally perplex.
He rubs his cheek and seems about to cry.
"Take it, you little silly! Don't they teach
you kiddies to say thank-you in this place?"
He snuffles and withdraws a pace or two.
Now Mrs. Delmer shows the chocolates:
row upon row, some gay with silver foil.
"Which will you start on, Derrick? This? Or this?
I should begin with this big pretty one.
I think it's strawberry. Look, I'll have one first."
She chews it with a show of great delight,
then swallows, beaming. Next she takes its twin,
pops it in Derrick's mouth with coaxing wiles,
inwardly praying that he will not spit.
His jaws begin to work; his hang-dog look

is suddenly transformed to confidence.
Now Mrs. Delmer wafts the bright balloon
trailing the string and blowing. Here and there
it wavers with delightful curveting.
And next she loops the string round Derrick's wrist,
then, bending, puts her ear close to his mouth,
to rise triumphant, clapping her plump hands,
"He's said his thank-you! *Hasn't* he been good?"
"I never heard him."
"But he did say—'ta'. At least he whispered.
You did, didn't you, Derrick?" Derrick nods.
"You say so, Madam. I must take your word."
"You like it, Derrick? It's a nice balloon?"
He nods again.
Then suddenly a gust of passionate love
sweeps through his being:
he takes the scarlet treasure in his arms,
clutching it to him.
Alas, the warning comes too late, too late!
There is a bang that makes poor Derrick start,
and at his feet
a worthless squiggle of damp rubber lies,
mocking late glory.
Derrick's face turns red, then pales to ashen.
Fiercely he grinds the ruin with his heel,
then spits upon it.
"Oh, temper! Temper! Dirty little beast!"
"Oh, *please*, don't let him think you mean to
    strike him!"
"As you wish, Madam."
(The nostrils have gone white; the eyes are steel.)
"But when I have him with me, he must learn.

Yes, even in *your* house he'll have to do
what *I* insist on. I won't have him spoilt."
When Derrick hears 'your house', he turns his face
up from the rubber squiggle.
He stares at Mrs. Delmer. In his eyes
is the same look that shone in them when first
they rested on her. Mrs. Delmer draws
the water-colour from its tissue sheath
and shows the dormer window, jasmine framed.
"That will be your room, Derrick."
He stares, uncomprehending. "There will be
a pretty lady in the house as well:
Miss Lettice, you will call her. She's so kind.
You'll love her, darling."
                                        Now their time is up.
The grim attendant swoops to sweep him off.
"A kiss? You'll let me kiss you?" Derrick nods.
This time he does not rub the kiss away.
He tags along, gripped by authority,
turning his head to stare as he departs,
fixing his gaze on Mrs. Delmer still.
He does not wave in answer to her wave
nor does he smile. But nor does he forget;
his thoughts dwell on her, as her thoughts on him
while she jolts homeward in the cable-tram,
with Flora opposite.
'He's like a tender seedling,' she reflects,
'feeble yet healthy, pale for want of sun.
Lettice will coax him happy.
Seedlings need kindness: that's what Lettice said
to the new garden boy. . .
You've got to love them, coax them, make them feel

that they are wanted.' Mrs. Delmer's thoughts
are broken into sharply. Flora Tort
rouses from *her* reflections on the boy,
and gives them utterance. "Not a pretty child.
I'd hoped that he'd be curly, with big eyes.
He's skinny, too. And, Madam, don't you think
he's got a squint?
And shocking manners. Even when he's trained
I wonder if I'll like him much . . I *may*. . ."

* * * *

"Mama, come now! They're ready. Oh, do come!
I'll show you Flora's first, and then the boy's."
With silk skirts raised—the attic stairs are steep—
the mother hastens.
Lettice has had her own way with the rooms.
Her taste, though not her hands, controlled the brush
that spread the rose-pink paint and moss-rose paper.
Her taste, though not her hands,
determined that the frills edging the curtains
must needs be gathered softly.
"Goffering is much too stiff. That dear old semptress
misunderstood and goffered them at first.
I hated giving her the trouble
of doing them again. But she was sweet:
she said it was a pleasure to oblige me.
I'm sure that Flora'll be a different person
living with us among these dainty things.
Even the soap is pink! Geranium. Sniff.
It's much less crude than pink carnation."
(Remembering the smell when Flora sneezed
into her handkerchief, her mother thinks:
'Would Flora have liked pink carnation best?

—But Letty will develop Flora's taste,
not pander to it.') "Darling, it's exquisite!
How right to say I mustn't have a peep
till everything was done!" "Now Derrick's room!"
(Buttercup yellow, papered with Tom Thumb,
and Tom the Piper's Son and Tommy Tram,
dancing together.)
"I bought the dearest little primrose brush
to match the tooth-mug; afterwards I thought
perhaps there'll be a toothbrush with his things,
and to provide one might seem rather rude,
at least not tactful." "Dear, of course you're right!
I should have put the brush beside the mug
and hurt her feelings." "—I can hear the cab!"
Eager and lissome, Lettice runs downstairs,
breaking her journey to snatch up her purse,
to pay the cab-fare.
Derrick stands clutching Flora's well-cut coat.
He scowls at Lettice. He is smartly dressed:
a midget middy,
H.M.S. Dreadnought on his cap, and dread
written, no less insistent, in his stance.
The week that's ended has bemused his wits.
(Nights in a feather-bed with Flora Tort,
days in vast West End shops, cream-buns and slaps,
jostlings and vomitings. . .)
Lettice has kneeled, coaxing with proffered toys.
He stares at Martha,
who, proffering no blandishments, is not
provocative of fresh malaise or turmoil.
In the past week proximity has roused,
feebly and fitfully, maternal love

to combat Flora Tort's contempt for squint
and scowl and knock-kneed scarecrow legs
and mute suspicion.
"You must excuse him, Miss; he's very tired.
Besides, it's all so strange." "Of course it is!"
Lettice springs up at once with graceful ease.
"He wants you to himself! He'd like his milk
and biscuits in your room while you unpack.
We will make friends tomorrow."
She is too wise to grasp the middy's fist.
She leads the way, still chatting.
On the top stair, praying for fortitude,
her mother waits. "Oh, Madam! What a room!
Why, everything is *lovely*! Derrick, look!
Look at your soap! A *pup*! Look at the mug
to use with your new toothbrush!" Flora stands
gazing about her, genuinely touched.
But Derrick, overwhelmed, begins to cry.
His hostesses withdraw,
mouthing their understanding sympathy
to Flora, who, relieved to see their backs,
searches for aspirin and slaps her son.

* * * *

Derrick's eyes are red, his pale face swollen.
He sits and squints next day at morning prayers,
Flora looks troubled too.
Excited scolding from upstairs has grieved
Lettice and Mrs. Delmer. Hulbert's frown
is fierce with disapproval. Rendell reads
the Scripture portion imperturbably.
He hopes the plan will prosper, knows the risks,
views Flora as a fellow-sinner, good

and bad, like Hulbert and himself,
like Lettice, even like his wife—adored
but not a haloed saint.

Now all but Derrick—he has not been pressed
on this first morning—kneel and join their hands,
murmur Our Father, Martha just a shade
behind the others, as she always is,
part in meek deference, part
from natural ineptitude, perhaps,
for anything but cooking and goodwill.
The Delmer's breakfast has preceded prayers.
Now from their knees all rise; the men depart:
Hulbert to hospital, wrath in his breast,
Rendell (first kissing Lettice and his wife,
nodding to Flora, patting Derrick's head,
this unrebuffed by the clench-fisted child),
to his consulting-room in Harley Street.
Flora is deftly stacking plates and cups,
"How clever, Flora! Everything just right!
Why, you remembered every word I'd said:
each little detail."
"Oh Madam, if the Master's satisfied
—and you—I'll work my fingers to the bone.
You can't think what it means to have this chance."
Lettice is coaxing Derrick with a grape;
but Derrick stands suspicious and withdrawn.
Flora puts out a hand;
Derrick accepts a finger. As he goes,
unseen by Flora he extends a tip
of hostile tongue at Lettice and her smile.
"Oh, the pathetic little misery!

Mama, we'll have to love him *such* a lot
to make him love us. But he will, I'm sure.
Indeed, he does already, I believe,
love *you*, my darling!"
Later, on the stairs,
when Mrs. Delmer's seen her daughter off
to spend the morning at a sketching-class,
there is a meeting, painful to them both,
of maid and mistress. Flora's arms extend
round Derrick's bed-things. "Madam, I can't think
what you will say... Don't tell the Master, please.
It's training, Madam. I have whipped him well.
It shan't occur again: I'll see to that.
And such a lovely little mattress too. . . ."
The acrid smell from Flora's burden strains
the sympathy her mistress tries to show.
The little mattress once was Lettice's,
then always stainless.
It does occur again. Such accidents
mar many mornings. Frequent pilferings, too,
astonish Mrs. Delmer and enrage
Flora, whose whippings bring no penitence
and no amendment.
Lettice's hair-slide and her trinket-box,
her pale jade ornament, her sealing-wax,
are found in Derrick's play-box, in the loft,
and in the hen-house. Mrs. Delmer pleads
for fewer whippings and more gentle tales
of Jesus and His love for little boys.
Silent, a cunning shadow, day by day,
he gulps her stories, sniffs her proffered flowers,
but does not cease to pilfer or to wet

the little mattress. Tantrums, too, persist.
One day when Lettice brings her latest sketch
and by her coming interrupts a tale,
Derrick sets up a roar, and rudely tugs
at Mrs. Delmer's frock until he rends
the gathers from the band.
He spits at Lettice, who, controlled but firm,
seeks to restrain a passionate assault
on shin and ankle.
Lettice and Mrs. Delmer now withdraw,
leaving him roaring. Mrs. Delmer gasps.
"I fear we've failed . . . I think they'll *have* to leave.
The life's so different. It is too much strain
for him *and* for his mother. . ." "Dearest, no!
It's want of confidence, I truly think,
that keeps him so resentful.
I've watched poor Flora hold a stick—quite low—
and try to make him jump.
It seemed as if he were afraid to raise
both feet at once in case when they came down
the earth would not be there!"
For once the daughter finds her words ignored.
"I think we'll *have* to tell your father, dear.
Flora keeps pleading, but I think we must.
Surely he'd say the time has come. . . And yet
I shrink from troubling him." "Of course you do!
Daddy has so much on his mind just now.
It will be better when it's all fixed up.
After we've moved, he will be free to help.
He might take Derrick fishing. I'd go too,
to see he wasn't harassed."
Habitual adoration sways once more.

"You're so courageous, Letty. You're so *wise*."
"Come and lie down, my precious. You are pale.
That scene has made you shaky." "*You* must change:
your're dining with the Conways, don't forget."
It is an hour before they meet again.
In Rendell's dressing-room, on Rendell's couch,
tired Mrs. Delmer has composed herself,
and listened to a book read soothingly;
now *she* must change for dinner.
She meets her daughter, come to say goodbye.
"Darling, enjoy yourself." ('How sweet she looks
with that cloak drawn about her slender arms!
—Although she scarcely needs it in this heat. . .')
"Tell Francis I'm *so* pleased to hear his leave
has been extended." "Don't wait up for me:
I promised Francis I would go with him
to listen for a nightingale. I may?"
"Of *course* you may! Hulbert will let you in."

* * * *

"You're awake, Letty? Such a lovely day!
Was it a pleasant evening? Did you hear—"
Letty, still sleepy, reaches up to hug.
"—Lettice! Dear child! That mark?"
(A little horse-shoe, scarlet, on white flesh.)
"*Derrick*? He didn't *bite* you?—Oh, he *did*!"
"I meant to keep it hidden . . . I believe
that he was sorry he had torn your frock:
I found him sitting on the stairs, his eyes
fixed on the door, waiting.
I knew that you were tired. . . I led him off,
and talked—and then I stooped,
meaning to kiss him.

He lost control completely, bit and scratched—"
"Your father'll *have* to know. T't, there's the gong!
Hulbert will want his coffee. Oh, my dear . . ."
"Don't worry, darling! It will all come right."

* * * *

The weeks pass by, with ups and downs—and ups.
Derrick seems less disturbed: perhaps because
Dr. and Mrs. Delmer have both shown
that though so naughty he has been forgiven.
(Flora has not been told about the bite
—or the torn gathers.)
Rendell's affairs are settled. Hospital
and Harley Street begin to seem remote.
Thoughts centre round the life that lies ahead,
in a West Country village. Foursquare House
seemed to him home at sight: a friendly place.
It's plain his work is finished; he's content
to vegetate, God willing. (One year? Two?)
Not till the date for moving has been fixed
are the domestics told about the plan.
Martha, a country woman, is unmoved,
but not so Flora Tort. She lies awake,
swears at the cuckoo, gulps down aspirin,
for once is late with breakfast; drops the milk;
says a bad word beneath her breath; then weeps.
Hulbert, in icy rage and breakfastless,
departs in silence to his hospital.
Lettice mops up the milk. "Flora, don't cry;
ask Martha for more milk." "Oh, Letty dear,
take Daddy's medicine to him and explain."
Lettice explains to Rendell, and stays on

—her hand still on the door-knob.
"She's torn in two, I fancy. I can't see
Flora in Pagnell Parva. No bright shops,
no moving pictures. Yet she knows, *must* know—"
"Send her up, Letty." Rendell interrupts
a trifle sharply. Lettice is not pleased
to be cut short. She mutters sulkily:
"I hear her coming with your breakfast-tray."
Flora's red-eyed, but competent again.
Lettice would like to stay, but must withdraw.
"You find our news upsetting, Flora, eh?"
"Oh, Sir, I know I couldn't stand just grass:
just grass and ducks. . . But I should never find
another place like this, Sir.
He's seemed more settled, Derrick has, of late.
And now I've had him with me I don't want
(at least I think I don't)
to pack him off to wear a pinafore
a mile too large. . . His hair's begun to grow;
it's got a shape. . .
And if I took in sewing; lived in rooms,
I'd *murder* him one day! I nearly did
that time back in the spring. It's *hell*—no less,
having a child around you *all* the time:
and one who squints, too. Here, it's different.
He loves the Mistress, and he'll stay with her
hour after hour. She's taught him little songs
that she's made up. She tells him fairy-tales.
I haven't got the knack, Sir. Oh, the days
would be so *tedious*! And then, the nights.
I couldn't leave him . . . Yet I know I *should*.
I'd get in trouble, Sir. Oh, I'm ashamed. . ."

She turns aside and bites her lip, and weeps,
while Rendell sips his coffee, sips and waits.
"I've managed to keep straight, Sir, all this time
because of you, and knowing that you cared.
I'd never keep it up, not on my own."
"Give Wilts a trial, Flora. You might find
the country isn't only grass and ducks.
You mightn't hate it."
Meanwhile, downstairs, Lettice expounds her views.
"I realise, Mama, you'll be quite *glad*
if Flora leaves us. Well, *I* think you're wrong.
I'm sure you'd miss them. Derrick's come to count.
(Hulbert had gone to Harrow, hadn't he,
before you knew him?)
And now with Daddy poorly it's a help
to have a really well-trained parlourmaid.
Why, even Hulbert owns that she's *efficient*.
Annie never thought
of seeing that the boot-boy shined the bits
between the sole and heel,
or put new laces when the old ones frayed.
And think how good she is at laundering!
She does the little dainty things *so* well,
and all the tea-cloths Annie used to send
to Mrs. Bonner—"
"Lettice, I will not have dear Annie blamed
when she's not present to defend herself."
"I *didn't* mean to vex you. . . Kiss me, please.
And say I am forgiven." "Letty *dear* . . ."

* * * *

"Hulbert, he's really better? You are sure?"
Lettice has been excluded from the room

where Rendell Delmer has lost consciousness.
Hearing her brother's footsteps on the stairs,
she follows anxiously.
"The attack's over. He needs rest, of course.
You get upstairs to bed.
Mater will call me on the speaking-tube
if he should wake in pain." "Flora's not back."
"I'll let her in. You're looking pale. Don't wait."
"Oh, I'm all right!
But if I stayed down here, Derrick might wake
and no one hear him call. Martha's asleep."
Hulbert sits reading for an hour or so.
He has forgotten Flora. His lids droop.
There is no sound from speaking-tube or bell
to rouse him from his dozing.
He stirs to hear the hall clock striking three.
There comes a scrabbling; then the sash is raised.
Hulbert pulls on the gas which he'd pulled off,
but for the pilot, from economy.
The mantle glows. "*Flora*!—You know the time?"
"Oh, Sir, it's never been this way before. . .
I'd hoped I'd slip upstairs and no one know
—and yet I knew I couldn't."
Hulbert's voice cuts her; it is steelier
than she has known it. "Get upstairs. Be off.
Go on your stockinged feet. Your Master's worse."
"Oh, Sir! A heart turn? Is he very bad?"
"Too bad for him to hear what would disturb
    him.
Tomorrow you must give your notice in.
Now go—you whore."
The word surprises Hulbert. It has leapt

without his willing it, through his clenched teeth.
Flora slinks by him, speechless.

* * * *

Inklings of change have seeped through to the child.
He asks no questions, only sticks more close
to Mrs. Delmer, only looks more pale,
only scowls more, squints more.
Lettice reflects that though it is weeks now
since he has pilfered,
it would not be surprising—the poor scrap—
if in this atmosphere of change to come,
with Flora strained and edgy, he should fall.
It does not, then, surprise her very much
to miss a nightgown from her chest of drawers,
a sovereign from her purse.
She finds him squatting at her mother's door.
He seems less hostile than she feared—less strained.
She leads him to her room, and draws him close.
"I am not angry with you—but I'm sad. . .
I want you to put back the things you took,
just where you found them. No one knows but I,
and no one *need* know, Derrick, if you do."
Derrick goes tense, and then he snatches up
a fragile bottle,
hurls it at Lettice, sees blood bead, blood flow,
flings himself down, bangs with his head, and screams.
There is a thud of footsteps on the stairs.
The door bursts open.
Flora grips Derrick by his scrawny neck,
shakes him, then wallops him, then shakes again.
"What's this, you little bastard? Hold your noise!
Oh, I'm fed up! Fed up!

You get away before I murder you—"
Lettice protests. —Then gasps, her startled eyes
focussed on Flora's bosom.
Within the gap of the unfastened blouse
she sees a camisole her mother made.
Flora shoves Derrick stairward; slams the door,
tears off her blouse, and then the camisole,
and hurls it from her. "Oh, my God! *I* took
your bloody nightgown and your bloody cash!
I've never taken anything before.
But now—I'm done. I'm ill again. I'm ill.
I'll have to go to that foul hospital.
I'm ill, I tell you."

* * * *

Mrs. Delmer stoops
over her washstand. She has nothing on
except her drawers.
"*Derrick*!" Her deep flush spreads. "You didn't
knock!
Bad boy . . . *Bad* boy!
Go to your mother. She must punish you."
Though wet, she has to sit, she trembles so.
Last night she did not sleep. Rendell was ill.
She needs a longer rest this afternoon
but has to cut it short. Bonner's to come,
bringing her daughter to be interviewed.
(Cherry is young but stalwart;
and she was brought up in the Manor House
where Bonner was a well loved stillroom-maid
after her husband's death.)
Flushed Mrs. Delmer dries and clothes herself.
A knock, an urgent knock. Flora bursts in,

not waiting for permission. "I must leave.
I'll have to go. Now. Now. This very day.
I'm ill. My nerves are dreadful. I can't wait.
I've packed. My things, *and* Derrick's. Workhouse
brat. . .
I'll have to go to hospital again.
Why did you have me here? You didn't want me.
You never liked me. It was all for Christ . . .
I hate you. *Hate* you."

* * * *

Here are the Bonners coming up the drive;
they carry a great basket of washed clothes.
"Why, Mummer, there be Derrick, all alone,
running as if a dog was after him."
The mother, less long-sighted than the girl,
peers as she sets the basket on the ground,
then hurries forward.
Into her arms sinks Derrick. Like a bird
his heart-beat flutters. Mrs. Bonner runs,
holding him firmly, to the lily pond.
Kneeling, she cups her hand,
slooshes his tense-drawn face, his wrists, his neck,
until his breath comes: with the breath a sob.
Cherry looks on, perplexed by his distress.
"Shall I go fetch his mummer?"
At once he stiffens, panic in his eyes.
"Miss Lettice, then? Or may be Missus?" "Naw!
be nubbody he's wanting, not as yet."
By looks the mother bids the daughter go
to say she has the child. As Cherry goes,
Lettice comes seeking Derrick,
harassed, and wondering what to say that won't

incriminate his mother. She has tried
to bandage her cut wrist, but the blood seeps.
She keeps it hidden.
"The little lad's upset: I dunno why, Miss."
Derrick sights Lettice, screams, and clings to Bonner.
Humiliated, Lettice turns away,
for once uncertain what it's best to do.
Hulbert and Conway come, from Conway's club,
where they've been lunching.
She goes to meet them. "May I have a word
with Hulbert? You don't mind?" "Of course I don't."
Conway draws back and lets the Delmers pass.
He has not seen the blood, but senses trouble.
He feels uncertain whether to go home
or wait about.
And now he notes the basket, notes the girl,
notes Mrs. Bonner with the troubled child.
He offers help; Cherry's smile dimples thanks.
The man and girl match well: the basket swings
level between them as they stride, in step.
Though they have never met until today,
they might, he thinks, have often walked linked thus.

* * * *

Hulbert is bandaging the wounded wrist,
finding some outlet for his passionate wrath
in work that needs his skill.
His white-hot rage is tempered by relief
when Lettice adds that Flora Tort has packed.
"She's packed the brat's things too?"
"Derrick's things too." The name rebukes the 'brat'.
"She takes him back to where she brought him from?"
"She says she means to—Hulbert, it's all *wrong*. . ."

"The best place for him. Little guttersnipe:
he's cut your wrist—why, almost to the bone."
"I can't make out what has upset her so;
she's *ill*, I know, but why be so—*distraught*?"
Hulbert snips off the final bandage-tail.
"Wait till the Pater's better: don't ask me."
"We'll have to let him know she's ill again
and isn't staying out her month. Shall I?"
"Not you: I'll tell him."
Delmer sips his broth
and reserves comment till his son breaks off.
He contemplates the sorry happenings
without undue emotion.
"Tell Fuller he'll be needed, with the brougham.
I want you to see Flora safe inside.
If she's alone she may lose hope and yield
to some fool impulse. It's a painful job.
You'll take it on, though?" "Since you ask me to."
Hulbert controls his furious distaste
with a vast effort. "Bonner's girl stays here:
that frees her bedroom," Dr. Delmer adds.
"Bonner can take the child to Gospel Oak.
She'll mother him. She'll help him to forget.
Flora and he had best be kept apart.
Get Francis to bring round his motor-car
and take the boy and Bonner straightaway
—after I've seen her. She will need some cash
for food and so on. I can deal with that.
I'm troubled about Letty. . .
She isn't used to failure. We don't know
how Letty will develop. . . *You* must help.
Oh, I'm not dying now! But two years on,

three at the most, she'll need you. Get off now:
you've got a lot to see to." ('God! I *have*!')
Hulbert obeys his father, though he fumes.

* * * *

"So Bonner's got a little lad to love.
Never had one before.
Now as her Cherry's gone away to live
she'd miss her, but for Derrick.
No call for nubboddy to worry now
over that pretty nightgown what got lost.
Miss Lettice knows it wasn't Derrick's fault . . .
—And Derrick's mum, she's gone to hospital;
she's not too well, poor dear.
She's sorry she shook Derrick; it were just
as she were upset like, not being well.
Yes, and the Mistress:
she never knew as Derrick were upset.
She thought he'd bust in, naughty, so she spoke
a deal more sharp nor what she woulder done
had she but known, see.
Now Derrick's going to sleep, in Cherry's bed,
with Cherry's clock to cuckoo him awake
when Bonner brings his breakfast:
a bantam's egg, a brown one, honey too,
from Bonner's bee-skep. Derrick had a ride
—the only little lad as Bonner knows
as ever had one—in a cab with wheels
but never a gee-gee!
A lucky lad be Derrick! And he helped
do up the box with Cherry's clothes an' all
for Mr. Conway to take back to her,
now as she's gone to live where Derrick lived

afore he come to Bonner." On it flows,
the soothering and the solace.
She cannot leave him till the cuckoo clock
has cuckooed midnight, heard by her alone,
for Derrick lies relaxed, all tension eased,
sleeping so deeply that she creeps away
to make herself some tea and get some rest.

* * * *

Lettice is standing, heavy-eyed and pale,
holding the fragments of a feather-boa,
once dainty as its owner's silver hair,
now soiled and scrabbled. Mrs. Delmer comes,
as pale and heavy-eyed. Neither has slept
through the sad hours of darkness.
The drowse that followed dawn was irked by dreams.
Dreams of brave scarlet globes that shrivel, limp,
were Mrs. Delmer's, while her daughter dreamed
of shameful scarlet stipples on white flesh,
base stigmata made proud by mordant pride,
and owing nothing to that emptying
of self that fills the emptiness with joy.
The dreams, not understood, have wearied her,
left her perplexed and fevered. Her malaise
has been exacerbated by the sight
of Mrs. Delmer's ruined feather boa.
"Mama, I found it, just now, on the mat.
She must have flung it down, torn into bits,
then spat on it, and trod it."
Disconsolate, subdued, the mother stands,
plucking strayed silver feathers from the hair
and from the heaving bosom of the girl,
not knowing that she does so.

"She said I served her only to serve Christ.
Oh Lettice, she was right!
The Christ with*in* her soul I never loved,
I never saw. . ."
Lettice thrusts off the question: 'Was it Christ
I served her for?
(The Christ within her, *or* the Christ without.)
Did I not, rather, serve her in desire
to feel myself her patron, wise and sweet
and understanding?'
She puts her arms round Mrs. Delmer's neck
and croodles facile comfort. "It is wrong
to blame yourself, my precious.
We did our very best. All's over now:
we can forget it."
She gathers up each fragment of the boa,
runs to the dustbin, thrusts the fragments in,
and rams the cover down, yet finds all day
traces as light as gossamer disturb
her spirit with a leaden touch, a threat
of mirky penance. Hulbert's fingers, too,
pick at a floating remnant of the boa
vexing his nostril as he eats his soup
—aloof and sombre, dignity disturbed
by tickled membrane and a sudden sneeze.
He dines alone with Lettice, waited on
by Cherry, frowning anxiously as yet
under the burden of the new routine
that Lettice teaches. Hulbert does not speak.
He is still smarting from the ignominy
of Flora's transport to the hospital,
driven by Fuller, supervised by him.

'The whore . . . the harlot. . .'
Hulbert had felt the words within his throat
rising like bile to choke him yesterday,
and now again he feels them as he sits
opposite Lettice in her snowdrop dress.
"—Oh Miss, I'm sorry! On your damask cloth. . ."
Some drops have splashed there from the coffee-pot.
A form approaching by the garden way
towards the French window of the dining-room
has startled Cherry. "Come in, Francis, do!"
"You're just in time for coffee."
Cherry withdraws to fetch a cup, but first
her eyes meet Conway's eyes. The Delmers fail
to note her sudden flush—or Conway's tremor.
"We hoped you might look in." "Have a cigar."
"I didn't ask to see you yesterday:
I thought you'd both be busy." "You thought
right!"
(This, bitterly, from Hulbert.)
"I just left Cherry's things—and handed on
one or two messages her mother sent."
"Mama has had her dinner in her room.
She's tired after yesterday."
"It's not surprising." "I should think it's not!"
Bitterness breaks again, ignored by Lettice.
"Was the child crying still—at Gospel Oak?"
('Cherry's slow,' thinks Lettice.
She does not guess that Cherry is delayed
by strong emotion that must be controlled
before she dare touch egg-shell coffee-cups
in Mr. Conway's presence.)
"Well— he *was* crying, but less wretchedly.

He helped pack Cherry's night-things. —But
your wrist?"
Francis has only just remembered it.
"I had to put five stitches," Hulbert growls.
"She'll always have a scar."
"Oh, it will soon be better!—Cherry, wait
and take the coffee and the sugar-bowl
to Mr. Conway." Cherry's steady now.
She does not look at Conway. As she goes
Conway's looks follow till the door has shut,
softly, behind her.

*   *   *   *

The Delmers' clock strikes four. Mown grass
smells sweet.
Ducks quack and gobble.
The afternoon is sultry. A good day
for fishing, where the stream is overhung
by sallows, and the over-lapping stones
cranny the stippled trout until they dart
to snap, and tug, and twitch, and tug again.
"You've not forgotten to pick up your pills?"
"I've got them, little fusspot!" Rendell's voice
is kind and tranquil and affectionate.
"*You* won't forget to send the money off
to Mrs. Bonner?" "I am sending it
by Letty: she'll be seeing her so soon.
I wrote to Cherry yesterday to say
which train we should expect her by; and said
Miss Lettice would be taking this month's board.
Cherry's holiday seems longer than two weeks.
It will be good to have her back, dear girl."
"It's time she came. Letty is getting fagged."

"The war has been a strain for her." "So've I."
"Oh Rendell, I'm so thankful that the move
did what we hoped!" "God has been good to us."
"Hulbert exempt, you better, Francis safe. . .
I have been wondering: do you think this leave
—having dear Letty staying in the house—
will give the chance that Francis needs to clinch
their understanding?" "As I've said before,
I've never been convinced that there is one."
"Oh, Rendell, surely!" "Well it's two years now
since they have met. This leave should settle it:
either for on—or off." Now Lettice comes,
to fetch her father. "Come back in good time:
there's sewing waiting, Letty, don't forget.
That evening gown needs taking in, alas!
You've grown *so* thin!" Lettice makes no response.
She moves off listlessly. Her father sees
how little she desires to spend the hours
watching him fish beside the tranquil stream.
"You've packed some books as well as bait and tea?"
"I've read all ours." "You need a change, my dear."
"Wiltshire's all right. . ." (She has to raise her voice
to make it heard above the quacks and mower).
"But there are days when it seems—oh, too full
of ducks and grass. . ." Rendell has too much sense
to tease his daughter in her present mood.
He wryly thinks, but tenderly refrains
from saying, 'that's what Flora thought, poor girl.'
Instead he says: "Enjoy your holiday."
"Oh, I'll enjoy it! But the war—" She frowns.
"Francis right in it. Hulbert soon to be.
It will obsess them. And it's all so dull.

I don't mean dull exactly. . .
But I can't enter into it: pin flags,
study the papers and the maps each day.
I'm fond of Francis—oh, of course I am!
I wish we knew some people, though, with *brains*. . ."
Her father hesitates. At last he says:
"I hope you'll marry early. If you do
you *may* still want to paint and write—" "I *know*
you've got no faith in my capacity
for anything artistic and worthwhile:
you needn't say so!"
"I'm no art critic, Letty. I can't judge
how good your work is. Hulbert thinks it good.
Mama thinks all you do magnificent.
—I've talked too much. I'll have to stop a bit."
He takes a pill and soon can move again.
Lettice chokes back her rage and misery,
and walks in silence by him through the fields.
Daydreams obsess her when they've settled down
beside the stream. These do not bring relief.
Questions as well as daydreams throng the girl.
The problem Hulbert shelved is still unsolved.
"You'd better ask the Pater," Hulbert said
the day that Flora went to hospital.
Often since then she's tried—and failed—to ask.
But for his wife, Rendell would long ago
have talked to Lettice plainly, but her plea
has silenced him. "Letty's so innocent,
so young and fresh and pure, oh Rendell, don't!
I'll talk to her someday (perhaps) myself:
not about Flora (that's *too* difficult)
but I will try to make her understand

more than she does—or *should* as yet, dear child.
—But even later on, I may not try. . .
You were so wise, so gentle! Oh, I'm *glad*
that no one intervened and frightened me
before our marriage!"
So Lettice wrestles with her thoughts alone;
ponders, rebukes herself for pondering;
fumbles for something, *what* perplexes her,
though she supposes it is friends with brains.
When she has trailed home at her father's heels,
she finds herself, self-pitying, too fagged
to take those seams in as she meant to do.
"Bother the dress! I'll do it in the train."
Unthanked, the mother sets to work on it
while Lettice drags herself upstairs to bed.
'She's done too much while Cherry's been away.
Domestic work is not dear Letty's forte. . .
But what a mercy she can have this change!
She'll come back happy—as she used to be.
Why, it's quite likely she'll come back engaged. . .'
She lays the dress in tissue paper folds
and creeps to bed at midnight.
She's up betimes next morning; Lettice, though,
is late for breakfast, lets her mother pack
(although ashamed to do so), serves the lunch
perfunctorily. "Cherry will be here
to serve your dinner." Cherry comes at two.
An hour later Fuller's at the door
to fetch Miss Lettice for the London train.
"He's come too early. I shall have to wait,
yawning, at Pagnell Magna.
Old Porter Bill will hang around and wheeze."

"*Fuller* can wait, dear. Stay and chat with me."
Listless, the girl pulls on her gloves. She pouts.
"What is there left to say? As well be gone."
Her mother strokes her cheek and tries to smile.
"Goodbye, dear Letty. Have a lovely time!
Don't worry about Daddy. Give my love
to Francis and his mother, and dear love
to Hulbert. Tell him—" "Oh, I'm in a whirl!
So many messages. I shall forget."
"You're tired, dear. You should have gone before.
You need the change. And Francis—half his leave
is gone already."
"I *couldn't* go till Cherry had come back."
Lettice picks up her handbag and moves off.
"My darling child! I didn't mean you could!
You are too sensitive. . . Kiss me goodbye."
"Goodbye, Mama. I'm *sorry*. . . Spare yourself
now Cherry's back. She looks so strong and well
after her holiday." "She does indeed:
her lips are cherry-red to match her name!
—Goodbye, *dear* Letty!"

* * * *

Hulbert and Lettice trudge towards Gospel Oak.
"How queer it seems to be in Fitzroy Park
and not at Number Three!" The words break out
explosively from Lettice. Hulbert notes
the underlying grouch but lets it pass.
"I see the people who are living there
have had it painted." "Yes, an acid green.
Hideous, I thought it." "Take what you can get
in war-time, I suppose." The talk trails off.
Silence becomes oppressive. 'War again,'

broods Lettice. 'War, war, war. I hate the war.'
Many well known to Hulbert have been killed,
but no one near to her. She does not grieve
with godly sorrow; grudges; is ashamed
only to grudge, vexed at a selfishness
she can't eradicate, or thinks she can't.
"Bad luck that Francis has been called away.
—But it may mean promotion." "After all
it's only one day with him that we've missed.
And I would sooner get this errand done."
"Mater still sends the money for that brat?
I own I think it's folly."
"Flora has sent some sometimes. But it's dropped."
"It would, of course!"
"Derrick's forgotten us, so Cherry says."
"Has he, indeed!
No gratitude for all the kindness shown. . ."
The walking-stick in Hulbert's hand beheads
a weed with one incisive vicious swish.
"Let's talk of something more worth talking of."
They have already talked of Delmer's heart,
Lettice supplying first-hand scraps of news,
and Hulbert comment.

Lettice now begins—strained by displeasure—
to challenge Hulbert,
with a childish arrogance.
He listens crossly to her strident voice,
then snarls—though he's been longing for her—
answers that irritate her.
Sensitised by misery
(since he's not in khaki when he aches to serve),

flayed by the fear that death may snatch at
Francis,
Hulbert can scarcely bear his sister-critic
as she carps at him and nags him.
For Lettice insists scratchily
that aching to be in the war is a whim that merits
contempt.
"You are doing far better serving at home humbly
than seeking false glory, it seems to me, Hulbert,
out on the battlefield,
for unmarked, unpraised, wholly unheroic
home service
is, to my mind, *self*-satisfying or *not* self-satisfying,
much more admirable than a soldier's blatant
offering."
The feeling that wings her futile plea exhausts
the girl.
Never until now have brother's and sister's wills
so wretchedly tugged criss-cross.
Hulbert's need is passionate.
Male insistent impulse to seek security through
action urges him.
Like some sharp prick,
or some whip lashing him,
the desire to serve his country,
male-bonded, goads him on.
But war for Lettice dams, rudely and blatantly,
the need *she* knows.
Bitter thwarting,
hateful thwarting,
in war, for one concerned with personal talent.
Lettice is not drawn towards nursing.

Nor could the land attract a girl so squeamish as
to smells,
so reluctant to be soiled,
so easily fatigued.
The sundered two, each jarred to be thus sundered,
each perplexed at being at loggerheads,
trudge in heavy silence for the final quarter mile.
A lack, foreseen and trivial, eases the strain at last.
Hulbert's limp pouch demands a shop—ahead.

The Bonners' cottage is in sight by now.
Soon Lettice taps the open door, then waits.
No answer comes. She pushes and goes in.
Derrick is sitting in an easy chair,
nursing a cat.
He has a cushion on his bony knees.
Though they're still bony, he's no scarecrow now.
He stares at Lettice. "Mrs. Bonner's out?
How are you, Derrick? You remember me:
Miss Lettice, whom you used to live with once,
over at Highgate? Fitzroy Park, you know.
Or *have* you quite forgotten?" Derrick's gaze
rests on his *Comic Cuts*, not on his guest,
as though the only sounds within the room
were the cat's purring and the clock's slow tick.
Lettice surveys him coldly; then her eyes
rove round the room. They wander to the pair
of china dogs, the willow-pattern plates,
the picture of young Queen Victoria
with her Prince Consort.
Then from the corner of the picture-frame
a snap-shot hits her, like a pointed stone

slung from a catapult. On Derrick's swing
sits Cherry, radiant, and at Cherry's back
stands Francis, radiant too. Her tilted face
laughs in the face of Francis, tilted down.
The camera has wobbled. (Derrick's hand
released the catch.) But, though the snap is poor,
there is no doubt of the identity
of girl or lover. Lettice looks away,
controlling her first impulse to advance
and snatch the snap-shot from the picture-frame,
rend it, and toss the fragments in the fire.
She shuts her mind, determined to conceal
humiliation's torture from the child
and from herself no less.
She turns to Derrick. He is sucking sweets
and thumbing over *Comic Cuts*, withdrawn
and mutely hostile. He has caught a cold:
that is the reason he has stayed at home.
He snuffles blatantly, then draws his hand
deliberately across his snotty nose,
ignoring Lettice—and the handkerchief
pinned to his jersey. She, with flaming cheeks,
rounds on him fiercely.
"What a detestable small boy you are!
Rude and detestable and hideous!
As rude and hideous as you always were!
Well—it's no wonder you're detestable
when one considers what your mother was. . ."
She stops, appalled and terrified to hear
the words that seem to break from someone else
—not Lettice Delmer. Derrick sits and stares.
Then suddenly he flings the cat at her,

and next the fire-irons.
Lettice stands trembling; Derrick holds his breath;
they both are speechless. The indignant cat
darts through the open door between the feet
of its returning mistress, who, perplexed,
looks first at Lettice then at Derrick Tort,
whose eyes are squinting. Mrs. Bonner runs
and snatches from a corner of the room
a bowl of water. "Now then, laddie, cry,"
she bids him as she deftly ducks his face
into the bowl. He draws a breath, convulsed,
then sobs, and flings himself into her arms.
She carries him upstairs, while Lettice stands,
her eyes averted from the picture-frame,
her lips contorted.
She does not wait, but, with a shiver, turns,
slips from the house, and faints—as Hulbert comes
(his purchase made) to fetch her.

* * * *

Back in Fitzroy Park,
Hulbert sits writing letters. When they're done
he takes them to the post. On his return
he's met by Francis, troubled to have missed
the first hours of his visit. "No one's fault.
—It *is* promotion?" "Yes, your guess was right.
But, Hulbert, how is Lettice? Mother says
she isn't well. I'm anxious. . ?" "She's fagged out.
I got a cab to bring her back, and now
she's resting on her bed. But she'll be down
for dinner. I suspect that tiresome brat
was cheeky and upset her." "He's all right.
With Mrs. Bonner, and with Cherry too,

he's perfectly amenable. No doubt
he was upset because he didn't have
the ride I'd promised."
"You seem to know that household pretty well."
His friend's sardonic tone makes Francis flush.
"Hulbert, old man—I haven't had a chance. . .
Did Mrs. Bonner. . . Have you guessed. . . ? I say,
I do hope Lettice will not feel—let down.
How *can* I put it?" Hulbert's bearing grows
more icy with each phrase that Francis frames.
He will not help him: only waits, with lip
curled in a scornful twist. "It's Cherry, Hulbert!
I think she loves me, but she's holding back
because she knows my mother isn't pleased.
—I say, don't cut me!"
"Congratulations hardly seem in place,
but if you want them, have them." Hulbert turns,
lights up his pipe to shield his misery,
and stands averted. Francis lays his hand
on Hulbert's shoulder. "I say, Hulbert . . . please. . .
You make me feel a cur!—We weren't *engaged*
we never have been. I don't think she'll—*mind*.
She may feel like my mother. But, old man,
I don't believe she would have *married* me
if I had asked her." "Lettice has good taste
—and Cherry Bonner's choice, I hardly think,
would coincide with hers." "You *needn't* sneer. . .
—You're going to tell her? Or shall I? Decide."
"I've no ambition to impart the news."
"You're very bitter. Hulbert, we've been friends
since we were seven. Don't let's quarrel now. . ."
Hulbert seeks egress through the dining-room

as Lettice enters by the other door.
Francis steps out to meet her, hand outstretched.
"You're better, Lettice? Do forgive me, please,
for having to go off—" "I understood.
Your mother tells me Hulbert's guess was right.
Congratulations, Francis. Do I err
in thinking that perhaps I ought to add
congratulations on another score?"
It might be Hulbert speaking were the voice
that Francis shrinks from not a treble voice.
Francis attempts to deal with what it says
not what it shows:
its surface smoothness, not its bitter thrust.
"Lettice, my dear, I'm hoping—but as yet
Cherry won't let me say that we're engaged.
—Did Mother tell you?" "No, but I'm not blind.
I hope you will be happy, Francis dear.
Your shirts will be well laundered all your life.
Cherry's a splendid servant: not so good
as Flora Tort, perhaps, but better far
than dear old Annie."
Once more the phrases spurt from someone else,
it seems to Lettice, someone devilish.
Francis stands helpless. Lettice schools herself
and sheathes her weapon. "Daddy sent his love.
Mama as well, of course. . ."

* * * *

"Good-morning, Mrs. Bonner. You have come
to fetch your money?" "Oh, Miss Lettice dear,
it wasn't that I come for! No, I thought
as how you'd be so worried for the boy.
He's right today—or else we'd not be here.

He likes an outing dearly, and I knew
as Mr. Francis would be good to him
while I was with you."
Through the French window shouts and laughter
  come.
Derrick is chasing Francis on the lawn,
while Francis dodges. "We had understood
that he behaved himself much better now;
—but yesterday! I'd spoken to him kindly. . .
Well, you *saw*. . . And does he often storm
and hold his breath? It *must* be difficult."
Triumphant whoops come from the tennis-lawn,
and Lettice winces. "Never, Miss. Not once.
Not since I tucked him up in Cherry's quilt,
two year come August. Seeing you again,
it muster brought his mummer back to mind.
Though he's forgot her, something seems to work
inside his little heart if anything
to do with her come floating. There'll be times
he'll watch me sign the postman's slip as though
he had some sorter slimsy notion bob
up from his depths to say: 'That come from *her*,
or from the folks as knew her.' Then, may be,
he'll pinch some sugar, or he'll wet himself
(if you'll excuse me, Miss) afore he's right.
I takes but little notice, lets him see
I know he's done it: scolds him, loving like,
and he's himself again: plays with his puss,
or runs off to his swing. Soon he'll nip back,
not saying nothing, but to see I'm there,
and all as usual. He don't like things moved:
them china dogs, they've got to be just so,

about a handsbreadth from the willow dish,
or he's upset like. —Miss, I've chattered on
and never asked you how the Doctor is?"
Now penitent and now inexorable,
Lettice has wavered; almost brave enough
to let tears come—and truth.
But Mrs. Conway nears: the chance has gone.
"Oh he's much better, thank you. Don't forget
to take the money, Mrs. Bonner. Look—"
She *had* forgotten. Now she speeds away
glad to avoid the mother of the man
who wants to be her son-in-law in spite
of disapproval.
From the hall window Lettice sees her go,
welcomed by Derrick, though he's loath to leave
his game of dodge with Francis. As she nears
he wipes his nose (unbidden and serene),
for, though his cold is going, he still needs
to use the handkerchief pinned to his coat.
He does it deftly. Francis lifts him up
to Bonner's handlebars. Off the pair ride:
Derrick and Derrick's Bonner, both content,
back to the cottage, with its china dogs,
its willow-pattern dish, its purring cat,
its clock, slow ticking on the kitchen wall,
and Cherry's quicker ticking cuckoo clock,
by Cherry's patchwork-quilted feather bed
that now is Derrick's.

* * * *

Lettice has washed away the railway smuts.
Her mother has unstrapped the travelling-case
that Cherry has brought up—unthanked, but glad

to have Miss Lettice home. When Cherry's gone,
her mother kisses Lettice once again.
She takes her hands in hers and scans her face.
"Darling, I wish you didn't look so pale.
You shouldn't have rushed back; there was *no* need.
Cherry and I were taking every care
of Daddy. You were homesick, but, dear child,
your rest was far too short. Oh, *dare* I ask?
I have so wondered. . . . Francis: did he speak?
Did you refuse him?" "Yes, Mama, I did."
Never before has Lettice told a lie
to her mama: never a lie at all
to anyone, until by keeping back
the ugly truth, she lied at Fitzroy Park
to Mrs. Bonner. How shall she retract?
She had not meant to tell it. But it's told.
She falters for an instant, then breaks out:
"Oh, please don't let us talk about it now
—or ever! Surely it's enough to know
that I don't love him, never did or could,
but as a friend: a dear friend."
"You'll talk to Daddy, darling?" "There's no need:
Daddy has always known how I have felt.
Oh, please let's leave it!" "But poor Francis, dear,
how did he take it? Was he much upset?"
"He understands. There's nothing more to say.
I do not want to talk, or hear you talk,
of what has happened." "Dear, there's no one else?"
"Of *course* there isn't! What men do I see
but Fuller and the garden-boy down here?
Oh, and the Vicar! Is he eighty-one?

No, only eighty, I believe—" "My child!
You've never said such bitter things before. . ."
Words yet more bitter break from Letty's lips
in the sad weeks that follow. Cherry shrinks
from contact with Miss Lettice—whom she loves.
Martha alone remains invulnerable,
though she's disturbed by loss of appetite
in her adored young mistress. Rendell writes
to Hulbert in his grief. "Come if you can.
Letty is suffering. And I can't help.
She needs help now—and soon will need help more."
The premonition of his nearing end
fulfils itself. Next day he does not wake.
Lettice is stupified. She turns away
—hating herself for turning—from the grief
her mother puts in words that seem to her
too facile and too frequent.
She cannot cry. She cannot say her prayers.
Her heart seems ossified. She seldom speaks.
The hurtful weeks drag on. More and yet more
does Cherry seem a daughter in the house
(eager to serve and quick to note a need)
and Lettice less and less. Another blow
comes while the blow of Rendell's death is still
reverberating in the stricken house.
"Miss Lettice, come! Come quick! Summat's amiss!
The Mistress be took bad. She speaks as though
her mouth be full of cobweb, and her arm
and leg be gone all numb, like."
The pathos of the stumbling voice and mind
stirs pity in the daughter:
pity so piercing that she welds a shield

of inefficiency and bitterness.
Cherry's a nurse by nature. Lettice shrinks
from tasks that Cherry tackles in her stride.
The stalwart body and the willing heart
do what frail Lettice could not hope to do
and does not try to. Even slighter tasks
burden and tease her. Mrs. Delmer's cry
is always: "Sherry, Sherry! Where's she gone?"
when Lettice brings a washbowl or a tray.
The stricken patient, in her lonely bed,
fumbling and stumbling to express crude needs,
fails to express the love she vaguely feels
but can't so much as try to put in words.
Hulbert is grieved and helpless. His research
makes it impossible for him to spend
more than a rare few hours in the house
where his thoughts gravitate month after month.
In her black dress Lettice looks yet more pale
and yet more slender than in gayer clothes.
There are dark hollows under her grey eyes.
Her lips have taken a sardonic twist
that troubles Hulbert. He for years has known
in his own being trends he never thought
to see in his young sister.
"I can't believe it's doing any good
for you to stay down here. It's not your fault.
It's just the people whom they love the most
that patients in her state misunderstand.
It may pass off: quite suddenly perhaps.
That's much more likely if you go away
and leave her here with Cherry." "I go—where?"
"Come back with me to Chelsea. You could paint;

could go to concerts; sing, yourself; and write;
do all the things you've always longed to do.
I'd get you introductions, find you friends:
the sort of people whom you'd love to know,
who'd understand you."
"I'm certainly not wanted where I am."
Lettice attempts to seem detached and cool,
but her voice trembles.
Hulbert at last has won his Council's leave
to go as Army surgeon—but not yet,
for he has first to finish the research
that he's engaged in. "When I go to France
you could join friends in digs. Quite nice girls now
live on their own like that, so I've been told.
But probably by then Mater will long
to have you back, and you will want to come. . .
Lettice—I've never managed yet to say
that Pater wrote of you the night he died.
He said he hoped that I would help you through
if things got difficult." Emotion blurs
his sister's eyes, but she blinks back her tears
and tries to seem unmoved. "All right. I'll come.
You'd better tell Mama. There'll be no point
in drawing out the parting. . . Oh, I'm *tired*!"

* * * *

Though the late autumn is as warm as June
there is a fire in the bedroom grate
and the wheel-chair where Mrs. Delmer sags
is pushed close to it. Mrs. Delmer knits.
She's dropped a stitch, but doesn't know she has.
Her ball of wool escapes her. Hulbert stoops,
retrieves it for the second time, and tries

to put it where it can be kept secure
yet will revolve as needed. "It's no ushe.
You'll have to ring for Sherry." "But, Mama,
we've got to have our little confab first;
it's about Letty." "Letty's a naughty girl.
She doesn't try to help me as she should.
And she'sh unkind to Cherry." "But, Mama,
it can't be easy when you make it plain
that you depend on Cherry all the time,
and get so vexed with Letty." "She's shelf-willed.
She shouldn't have said no when Francis shpoke.
I'm sure she could have learnt to love him, dear.
She was pre-pre-preshipitate, and the poor man
on the rebound—it often happens so—
got this pre-preposterous idea that he
would like to marry Sherry. Sho abshurd."
"Mama, we've talked this out before, you know.
Don't let's discuss it now." "You'll make me cry
if you inshisht on teashing me like this."
"Don't cry, Mama. I only want to ask
if you'd allow Lettice to come with me
to Chelsea for a holiday."
"You must fetch Sherry, dear, I've dropped a stitch.
And don't come back; it tires me, all this talk.
Give me a kish, and go away, dear boy.
Yesh, Letty can go with you."
Hulbert bends down to kiss her. As he goes
he turns to wave goodbye. She does not look,
but sits immobile as an effigy,
one waxy eyelid drooped and mouth askew
wool in confusion.

* * * *

Lettice has waited, fuming, by herself
in the cramped restaurant near Hulbert's rooms.
She hesitates to order her own meal,
and watches for her brother.
At length she orders cutlet and green peas.
The meat is gristly and the peas are dry.
While she is picking at them gloomily
Hulbert appears, flustered and out of breath.
"*Hulbert*. . . ! So *late*. . ." "I do apologise.
I trust no one's annoyed you. I was kept.
A Council meeting. I was interviewed."
"That means you go—?" "As soon as I've
cleared up."
"And I'm to seek a hostel, I suppose:
be a young Christian Woman, or some such.
Ah, that's delightful!"
"What about joining Hester?" "She'd be bored.
And so should I, dear brother."
Hulbert had banked on Hester and her flat,
not knowing that the friendship had cooled off.
No other plan occurs to him; his face
falls and his voice shows his discomfiture.
"Lettice—I'm sorry." "Don't be *sorry*, dear.
You've got your heart's desire: if *I'm* marooned
what does it really matter? I'll go home
and learn to help old Martha peel the spuds.
Then Cherry will be free to spend *all* day
coping with slip-stitched knitting."
"Oh, don't be bitter!
I didn't tell you—but at the week-end
I found Mama was getting reconciled
to that odd *mésalliance*. The top floor—

it's to be made into a little flat. . ."
Lettice with shaking fork spikes two dry peas
and eyes them blindly. "What a charming plan!
Shall I go down and help prepare the flat
—as I prepared the rooms for Flora Tort
and her young hopeful? No, I think you said
to Francis—did you not?—some time ago
that Cherry's taste and mine would hardly click.
She will want china dogs and oleographs
of Queen Victoria." "Do try to *eat*.
That cutlet's cold. Let's send the thing away
and ask for something different." "You forget
that there's a war on. That is odd of *you*
when dipping fingers in the war-time pie
is all you care for." "*Lettice,* do control—
You're speaking rather loudly—"
He fumbles for a topic to distract.
"Tell me about the sketches. Did they sell?"
"They were not even hung: were crowded out.
Tonks came, and scorned them.
Oh, what does it all matter? I'm aware
I'm not an artist: just an amateur.
My wishy-washy water-colour daubs
deserve their fate. And I can't *sing*. My voice
—my little reedy voice—it's laughable."
"Don't be so angry with yourself: so fierce.
I've always thought your poems were the thing
that you were best at. Concentrate on them.
It may be best that you should realise
you need to narrow down your interests,
not dissipate them." "Well, I think you're right
about the poems. Soon I ought to hear

if Elkin Mathews means to take the book."
"You may have been quixotic to include
those simple little ditties of Mama's. . ."
"I thought Mama would like it: our two names
'Lettice and Lois Delmer'. . . I expect
she's really far too muddled to take in
the tribute now."

* * * *

The hostel bedroom, neat and comfortless,
its curtains not from Liberty's or Heal's
but from some cheaper shop that mimics theirs,
Lettice detests more violently each day. . .
The bed is sagged. The cubicle is hot.
Her book is heavy; soon her restless hand
flings it impatiently away.
"You're in!"
A face has peered round the half-opened door.
"Why shouldn't I be in?" "Miss Smithson thought
you'd asked permission to be leet tonate."
"And so I had." "I missed you from hay-tea.
I thought you might have started." "There's no need
to follow all my movements with such care."
"She's huffy now." Miss Hobley simpers, snubbed,
but trying to pretend she feels at ease.
Lettice relents. "My brother hoped to come
to take me to a concert; but he can't."
"*Some*one has come." "To see me, do you mean?"
"A most excating-looking someone, too."
Lettice is interested against her will.
Miss Hobley has her hands behind her back,
hiding a letter. Now she holds it out.
"He's brought a note. He *hoped* that you were in.

Ah-ha, dear!"
Lettice speaks coldly. "There's no need to wait.
(The letter's from my brother.) I'll come soon."
"Meanwhile *Ai'll* entertain the gentleman."
Lettice unfolds the letter.

> I hate to let you down. *I*'m disappointed. . .
> We'll get our farewell jaunt another day.
> Meanwhile do try to make the best of things
> I don't believe you meant to find a girl
> to use my ticket. Now I rather hope
> you haven't tried. I've met a man I know,
> or used to know at Harrow, and he's free
> (and eager, too) to take my place tonight.
> I've given him some money: there's no need
> to feel embarrassed when he pays for things.
> He used to be a decent chap at school.
> I hope it isn't rash.

She slooshes water on her tear-stained face,
which she has kept averted. Hulbert knows
—Miss Hobley mustn't—that she's miserable.
The disappointment, that is bad enough
but a mere dint compared to the abyss
Blackwell has dug for her.
She slips into her simple evening dress.
'The tickets, gloves, clean handkerchief, my purse.
—Why, I shan't need a purse!' She puts it down.
'I'd better take it. All these common girls:
one never knows. . .' She picks it up again.
(Only today she visited her bank
in readiness to pay her hostel bill.)
She starts to run downstairs, but checks herself.
She must not seem too eager.
She sees a man with lustrous eyes advance
towards the staircase, as Miss Hobley fades

reluctantly away to join the girls
who peer (and titter) from the drawing-room.
"A-ah!—Miss Letitia!" His bow is low,
elegant and respectful and discreet.
He holds an opera-hat within his arm.
Compared to Hulbert he looks young—and spruce.
His accent and his phrasing both suggest
the slightest trace of foreign ancestry.
"This is a *priv*ilege. . . I thought to spend
a solitary evening (I've just come
from overseas: a lonely ghost, a waif. . .)
And *now*—" …
A gesture takes the place of further words.
Appraising looks produce a sudden blush.
Lettice speaks fast to hide embarrassment.
"I know you just as Hulbert's friend. Your name—"
"I hardly dare accept the compliment
of 'Hulbert's friend': I was a humble fag.
Delmer I worshipped, as I made his toast,
almost as though he were a demi-god:
his strength, his brains, his status—" Once again
a gesture gives expression to a thought
that cannot find expression in a phrase.
He holds the taxi door and hands her in,
bowing as though she were a dignitary,
then enters with a reverential air,
respect embodied.
"And still you haven't given me your name?"
"Why, nor I have! It's such an *ugly* name
compared to yours. (Letitia: happy one!)
I'm Bois Diego (Dago-boy, of course,
to all the other scrubby little fags

when Delmer knew me.)—Miss Letitia,
have you a preference where we shall dine?
Or shall we try Pinoli's? Absently
I told the driver that's where we would go,
but we can choose some other restaurant
if you prefer?" "Pinoli's will be *nice*.
I've only been there once. The arty folk
in Chelsea took me out to restaurants
with frescoes on the walls done by themselves,
appalling cubist things. The tablecloths
were grubby—like their necks! Oh, I'm so *bored*
by those art students Hulbert thought I'd like.
The 'men' are merely boys. The men themselves
are in the services. And all the girls
wear smocks and sandals—and out*rage*ous hair!
They're just a clique who praise each other's work—"
She stops, and flushes.
She knows it would not seem a clique to her
if *she* were in it, if *her* work were praised.
She knows the boyish artists were hard-up,
their hospitality more generous
in that they shared the estimate of Tonks
as to her sketches. Her companion's face
shows no awareness of the shamed remorse
that has swept through her. Rather, it inclines
attentive and amused, as though her spite
were wit, and her ingratitude a sign
of insight into character that won
pleased commendation. At the restaurant
Diego wafts her on protectively,
in charge but deferential. "We'll sit here?
What may I order?" "Order for me, please.

I'm sure I'll like whatever you may choose."
He orders swiftly, expert and at ease.
"This *is* a treat! The hostel food—oh dear!
Of course I know it's war-time. How on earth
Pinoli's manage to produce all this . . ."
"Oh, there are ways. . ." "Hulbert is *most* austere.
So conscientious. . ." "Even in his teens
he had the conscience of a puritan.
I honoured him intensely. I was quite
a model boy in my first year at school.
I only knew him for one year, or else—"
"You might have been less—worldly, than you are?"
Already Lettice has begun to show
the influence of her escort's choice of wines:
her cheeks are flushed. Diego bows assent,
and in his eyes a glint of mischief shows.
She sees it and responds; her gay laugh peals.
Their mirth unites them. "Why, how quick you are!
You needed but a pause to take my point."
"Oh, poor old Hulbert!" "Is he rather—starched?
This Queen's Hall concert. . .?" "Hulbert's choice,
not mine!"
"You are less—highbrow, than I feared, perhaps?"
"Oh, *I*'m not highbrow!" Lettice finds herself
for the first time able to contemplate
without emotion words that for two days
and for two restless nights have tortured her.
That Lois Delmer's songs have 'a frail charm',
while Lettice Delmer's sonnets are 'derived'
and 'somewhat stilted' is irrelevant.
To prove herself a poet seems—tonight—
no more incumbent on her than to fly.

Classical music? Let it go to hell,
along with Blackwell's letter, printed slips
from Elkin Mathews, Constable, John Lane,
and Humphry Milford.
Again her glass is filled, again is drained.
"This highbrow music—shall we dance instead?"
"Just *cut* the concert?" "It's for you to say."
"I'd love to dance. . ." "You would? That's settled
then."
He folds the Queen's Hall tickets into boats
and sends them floating in the gilt epergne
beside the rose leaves.
"You'll have just one more glass before we go?"
"Oh, not *another*! It's not lemonade!
I'll have to take your arm or I shall *reel*."
"The air will help you. Such a pretty flush!
Ice-maiden into rose-bud. Steady now!"
He lets her sit in the cool vestibule,
and then he takes her to a dancing-hall.
Lettice is too much dazed to criticise
the ladies' low-cut dresses and the band's
raucous vulgarity. They sit, relaxed,
between the luscious waltzes. Lettice, flushed
and flattered, sips more wine, hardly aware
of what she does. "You steer divinely, Bois,
I've *loved* to dance. But not again." "Lean back,
against my shoulder." She leans back, and yawns.
He strokes her forearm softly. Soon her nerves,
taut with fatigue, produce a sudden jerk.
"Why, I was half asleep! It must be *late*.
Please take me home." "It isn't late, *ma chère*.
Before I take you back you need a rest.

There is a resting-room just over there.
Come, let me show you." "Oh, I am so *tired*!
I'd love some coffee for my shtupid head."
"I'll order something that will do it good.
The coffee here is vile."
She needs support to reach his resting-room:
a closet almost dark, its atmosphere
heavy with massed carnations.
She sinks into the cushions; does not hear
the waiter come and go, or the key turn.
"Sip this, my rose-bud. Oh, you look so sweet
with your hair fallen. Why, how long it is!
Lean here, and let me curl it round my wrist.
This divan's plenty big enough for two.
Lovely soft cushions."

* * * *

When Lettice stirs, bodily misery
precedes emotion. Throbbing head, and tongue
thickened and sour, bring acute distress
before her memory stabs her.
The unfamiliar slanting of the light
between the heavy curtains, and the smell
of wine and dying flowers bring her awake.
Bewildered, she stares round, then, terrified,
she wraps her cloak about her, snatches up
her purse, and flees.
She cannot find the exit, runs this way
and that. A night attendant beckons her,
points to the door,
and has it open for her when she comes.
He bows her out. She cannot look at him.
She fights her nausea and hails a cab.

Not till she pays the driver does she know
that one half crown is all that she has left.
She prays that she may slink upstairs unseen,
but meets Miss Hobley. In her cubicle
she tears off her white clothes, deep-stained with wine,
and yields herself to nausea.
The Warden comes, stern faced and scandalised.
Lettice lies prone, too wretched to look up.
Hulbert, she learns, has searched for her all night,
and still is searching,
distraught at what enquiries have revealed
of Bois Diego's post-Harrovian years.
Contact is made at last by telephone,
and Hulbert comes. She clings to him and sobs.
Her story tortures him; her shame is his.
The days that follow offer no relief.
Hulbert is forced to rush from this to that,
buying equipment, fitting uniform,
taking instructions, signing documents,
while knowing his young sister is alone,
utterly wretched and disconsolate.
He snatches moments with her when he can;
these do not cheer him.
At last the very day he is to sail,
he takes her for the farewell jaunt—postponed
with such disaster. Tacitly their choice
avoids a concert. At the matinée
(chosen by Hulbert with more care than skill)
they sit preoccupied and desolate,
trying to find some respite from their grief,
and failing, while the players strut and mouth
in would-be funny tedium. They adjourn

to an hotel for tea. (The Chelsea rooms
are let for the duration. Hulbert's club
makes no provision for a lady guest.)
The room is vast and chilly, the tea smoked,
and the toast sogged. "At least we are alone,"
says Hulbert with a sigh. " We *can talk* here."
He finds that she has planned a way of life
that horrifies him.
"But can't you see that I should worry less
if I could only leave you among friends. . ?"
"I simply *can't* go anywhere I'm known.
I must begin afresh." "It was *my* fault. . ."
"It wasn't, Hulbert. If I had explained
I wasn't used to wine. . . If I'd refused. . ."
She sees the tickets float in the epergne
and hears her foolish laughter. The tears brim.
"I've had such hours and hours to think and think.
It isn't only being such a fool
that dreadful night, that nightmare night. . ."
"My *dear*. . ."
"I've been so vain and selfish all along,
and so conceited." "Ah, don't cry, don't cry—"
"I need a new beginning. Let me *work*.
I've *played* at art and music.
And Blackwell's right: those sonnets *are* derived,
and more than *somewhat* stilted. And besides,
oh, I was *cruel*—to Derrick. (You don't know.)
And Cherry, I was horrible to her,
spiteful to Francis, hateful to Mama.
I lied to her, to Mrs. Bonner, too.
I know I've got to suffer, got to learn,
but it's too much to ask me to go home

and struggle *there* to be a better girl:
I just can't face it." "Mrs. Conway. . .? Try!
I'm sure she'd want to help you." "*No*body
who knew the hateful worm I used to be
can help me, Hulbert—except you yourself:
and you're committed.
I *can*not stay in Hart Street with those girls.
They saw me slinking in at breakfast time
in evening dress. When I go in to meals
they turn away. And *I* looked down on *them*,
and thought them coarse and common. . . Let me
work."
" 'Assistant Matron in an Orphanage':
You'd have to do such menial, paltry jobs.
I'd hate it for you." "Oh, I'll scrub the floors,
I'll wash the babies' napkins—anything,
if I can only be where nobody
remembers what I was." He yields at last,
reluctant and distressed. 'A better girl', he thinks;
'not used to wine'—why, she's a child; no more.
How *can* I leave her?' Miserably he says:
"You'll draw your own allowance just the same?
That ought to ease things." "No, I won't do that.
I'll draw enough to settle my account
at the Y.W. But I must learn
to do as other people have to do:
girls like Miss Hobley. When I saw my purse
(that dreadful morning), I thought: '*Other* girls
who haven't money in the bank—or friends,
what could they do?' " She blows her nose again.
Hulbert has ceased to listen. "Lettice dear,
one question while we're still alone." He sweats.

"You're sure you may not need to get advice
from some kind doctor, after that bad night,
that 'nightmare night'?" Bewildered, Lettice slips
her hand in his, and eyes him. "Hulbert, why?
A *doctor* couldn't help me. If one could,
why, you're the one to do it—and you do."
He probes no deeper, argues with himself
that had Diego raped her she must know.
Since she remembers nothing, there can be
nothing to be remembered—save the shame
of sleeping, drunken, in a stranger's arms.
He takes her to the writing-room and helps
her draft her application. She *needs* help. . .
He takes her back to Hart Street. His time's up.
He leaves with words that cannot voice his thoughts.
She, too, is halting in her loneliness,
but she chokes back her tears and tries to smile,

* * * *

Hulbert is on his way to Foursquare House,
on his first leave. He gives his ticket up
and passes on in gloom. He is surprised
to hear himself addressed by Mrs. Bonner.
Francis, she tells him, wounded in the foot
has come to Foursquare House to convalesce.
Since Cherry is with child, the work has proved
too much for her and Martha without help.
Letters to Hulbert have been misaddressed
and come back marked unknown. Cherry's afraid
that Hulbert may be vexed. " 'Go meet him, do',
she says, 'and tell him how it's come about
that you and Derrick's here.' "
All this he learns before they reach the cab

where Derrick waits, perched at the driver's side.
Much detail follows. Hulbert lends an ear
but is in part distracted by the thought
of meeting Francis.
He knows that Francis bears him no ill-will
for his harsh caustic words when they last met
at Fitzroy Park, but pride is slow to melt
in hearts like Hulbert's. Derrick leaves his perch.
He jerks the cab door open; makes a dive
for Hulbert's suit-case; staggers off with it,
red from the effort, obviously proud.
With swaddled foot and crutches, Francis waits.
"It's good to see you, Hulbert!" Barriers yield.
"It's good to hear your news!"
"Blighty—or baby?" "Baby. —Both, of course."
"If it's a boy you'll let him have your name?"
"If Cherry'll let him." "Cherry will rejoice."
Francis makes no suggestion that his friend
should stand godfather;
he knows that Hulbert could not make the vows.
Nor does he think it needful to proclaim
—today—that Bonner's Derrick is to stand,
supported by two grown-up godparents.
"How's Mater? Feebler?" "Well—at times, perhaps.
But most days she's quite chirpy: sings and chats
for hours to Derrick. He adores her still:
reads Henty to her half the afternoon,
deals with her tangled wool, and plays at drafts;
he's the best player, but she loses best
so both are happy.
—But, Hulbert, how is Lettice? Does she feel
that she's been ousted from her home by us?

That's our one dread: Cherry's and mine, I mean."
Hulbert is non-committal. Francis sighs.
He knows (and Hulbert knows he knows) that dread
is not without foundation. Nothing more
remains to say about it: both see that.
"Her mother hardly seems to grieve at all.
It beats me when I think what Lettice meant
to her at Highgate: how she worshipped her
and thought her faultless." "It's the stroke, of course.
It's rough on Lettice. —Lettice has changed, too.
They work her like a nigger at that Home.
I haven't seen her in the flesh for months:
I'm judging by her letters. We shall meet
on Saturday in London." "Difficult
to know how best to word our messages. . .
You put them into words. Try to convey
how much we'd love it if she would come home."
"I'll do my best. I only wish she would.
Well—it's a mercy Cherry's here; and now
her mother. Yes, and Derrick, so it seems!
It's strange to think that brat has altered so."
Hulbert's brief stay soon passes. All the time
his thoughts veer back to Lettice. Not a hint
comes from his lips of that disastrous night,
that nightmare night. His friend
senses calamity, but does not probe.
Hulbert would share the burden if he could:
that Francis knows—intuitive in all
that touches Hulbert. Mrs. Delmer seems
content to leave her daughter undiscussed
after one tearful grumble, querulous
but not embittered.

"You send your love, Mama?" "Of coursshe,
    of coursshe.
Letty's a naughty girl, but all the same. . ."
She drops her wool. "Send Sherry to me, dear."

* * * *

"Lettice! My child! You're far too thin, too pale—"
"A scarecrow with a secret: that's the phrase
that formed itself last evening when I stared
into the mirror, Hulbert.
Something a colleague muttered made me see
—I've learned so many things, vile things, from her—
why when we talked before you left for France
you hinted I might need a doctor. 'Kind',
that was the word you used.
Oh, what a *fool* I was! Oh, *what* a fool!
And now—I want your help. Find some 'kind' man.
He'll ease my fears, I trust, but—if he can't. . .
Diego—did you know he'd got two years,
for forgery? I saw it in the train
in someone's *Daily Mail.* A barrister
described him as 'a moral imbecile,
without a conscience.' 'Psychically unhinged
since adolescence—yes,' his doctor said,
'but *not* a moral imbecile: a man
charming but dangerous.' Those were his words.
Oh, Hulbert, answer! Don't stand staring there
as though you were a dummy in a shop.
You've got to *help* me."
But Hulbert cannot answer. For a while
he stares, as pale as Lettice, and as torn
by dread and shame and hope: *more* stunned
    than she

because he knows no comfort from the pad
that nature proffers with a side-long smile
even to anguished women when they breed.
An unwilled pregnancy finds salve of sorts
for bearer and begetter. Brothers smart
knowing no pad or unguent; doubly so
when self-blame's steel sharpens fact's cutting edge.
At last he mutters: "Two men come to mind:
give me an hour to weigh them. . .
What can I say? Oh, Lettice, curse me! Curse
if any comfort comes in cursing me."
"Comfort in cursing you? Hulbert, you're mad.
For Bois Diego not a curse would come.
No, I'm too tired for curses. God and I
may find ourselves no more on speaking terms,
but God himself I couldn't try to curse
—though He has let this happen. Commonsense,
you'd think, would have forewarned Him, on the eve
of making men and women, to curtail
their freedom—*or* their folly. *Both*?—It's mad!
Hulbert, the world seems—spinning. I must rest.
Make an appointment for me." Through the night
Lettice has travelled in a crowded train,
crushed between soldiers.
Her scarecrow secret has revolved in her
until her brain is reeling, and her lids
droop in their ache for darkness. She withdraws
to a drear bedroom in the vast hotel.

* * * *

Hulbert has weighed the two men in fear's scales;
one was his father's friend, bred in a manse,
upright, austere, a shade behind the times.

The other Hulbert nods to if they meet,
and knows well by repute. 'A coming man,
up in the latest techniques. She's not strong. . .
Less shame, too, with a man she doesn't know,'
he argues. There's been talk now and again
that he has disregarded, disbelieved,
frowned on as scandal. Yet a breath of doubt
has sometimes stirred, quelled almost as it stirred
—and quelled today. He goes to see the man;
finds him respectful, suave. . . . He hurries back:
finds Lettice paler.
He takes the telegram she thrusts at him.
Wounded and dying crowd his hospital.
He steels himself to leave her, takes her hand,
closes it round the paper with the name,
and the address, and the appointed hour
that she must go to Bromhead.
"Whether the verdict's good or—is not good,
do no more scrubbing, no more laundry-work.
You are not fit in *any* circumstance
to be a slave to brats like Flora Tort's.
Dear, if a child is coming—God forbid!—
rest, spare yourself. You *must*." "Oh, I will rest!
I'll do what*ever* Bromhead may advise.
Perhaps he'll know some guest-house that would serve
if I *should* need a refuge.
You wouldn't send me to him, I know that,
if he were not a person I can trust."

* * * *

Hulbert, in France, at his field-hospital,
by day makes bloody toil his torture's drug;
febrile at night he buoys himself on hope.

'She's sick with worry. Nothing else is wrong.
Bromhead will reassure her. I did right
to send her to a stranger.
Relief will bring ease from the whole distress.
She will forget Diego; she will learn
to make her home in peace at Foursquare House.'
Could he but pray, he would pray—with intense
and passionate fervour.
Petition—not for him. He cannot frame
petitionary prayers to a God
he only half believes in. Yet he knows
that if his urgent longings are fulfilled,
thanksgiving will break out involuntarily.
He has worked out the earliest possible hour
that he can hear the verdict. It goes by.
No letter comes the next day, or the next.
At last there's one. He tears it open; reads:

> I am alive.
> There's nothing more to say except—don't come.
> I don't suppose you could, but if you could,
> *I do not want to see you. Keep away.*

Embossed expensively, is the address:
a Nursing Home in Mayfair.
Hulbert is shaken by a tearless sob.
He curbs emotion, seeks compassionate leave,
is not refused, though his request brings looks
of shocked surprise.
Of his C.O.'s astonishment at claims
that fit so curstly with the circumstance
he hardly is aware.

* * * *

Lettice is propped on pillows, sapped and drained
of her vitality. A tray with food,

untouched, is at her side.
She stares, unseeing, through the windowpane.
The spire she stares at, traced on a blue sky,
means no more to her than the vacant wall
(blank as her mind) that frames the spire and sky.
She does not turn her head when a nurse comes,
but shuts her eyes. "Your brother's in the hall."
A shudder runs through Lettice, and her lips
wrench in contortion. "Shall I send him up?"
Again she shudders, as she signs assent.
His footsteps on the stairs dunt on her heart.
"Lettice! My child. . ."
"What have you come for? I said 'keep away'."
"I had to. *Had to*. Thank God you're alive!"
"I do not thank Him. Nor do I thank you."
"Bromhead—his doing?" "Yes. I gave consent.
I panicked and I gave it. Hulbert said:
'Do what this man advises,' that was how
I reasoned in my panic. Oh, God, God!
How could it violate so *much* in me?
So much I never guessed *was* mine—*was* me.
I take the blame. I let myself consent.
And so I must endure the—ignominy,
endure the loss. Yes, even Diego's child
is loss, I have discovered. Hulbert, go.
I know it must have cost you much to come,
but go, I tell you." Hulbert crouches, mute.
"Perhaps you didn't know the kind of man
this Bromhead is? Perhaps you didn't mean
that this should happen?—Though he thought
you did."
"I didn't mean to mean it. . ." "Surface thought

moved on a plane where good is good, bad bad,
and decency respected?" He can't speak.
"You must go back to your field-hospital
and do your best out there. There's nothing here
for you to do. And don't—don't be afraid.
I can't thank God that I am still alive;
but I shan't take my life."
"Lettice, go home! Let Mrs. Bonner help.
Let Cherry help—and Francis. They *could* help."
"Too much, too much! It is too much to ask.
Cherry with child, by Francis. (Oh, I know
I never loved him! But I thought him mine.)
Mama, preferring Cherry. Derrick there,
to be a thorn to prick me every hour
to smarts from sin I can't, no, *can't* forgive,
yet must forgive, unless I can forget."
"Lettice . . . my dear . . . some priest? Would that
    console?
I've heard men speak of sudden strange relief
coming in absolution." "No, no, no!
How could a priest absolve when God and I
are not on speaking terms?"
Words will not come, but Hulbert is convulsed
by tearless sobs that heave and torture him.
His sister trembles. "Don't grieve overmuch,"
she whispers hoarsely. Then new bitterness
breaks through compassion, and her voice
    grows fierce.
"I shall get plump when once I've left this hell.
Yes, it *is* hell.
The demon-nurses sneer or leer at sin.
Bromhead—his skilful fingers interlace,

arch-devil's fingers, manicured and smooth.
He comes and smiles at me each day at noon,
prescribing bromides.
He wears a mask of gauze. It veils his vice,
it doesn't hide it."
Suddenly she weeps, but quietly.
The bitterness fades from her misery,
but though she is not bitter any more
she is no child. Her woman's misery
batters at Hulbert (as she turns to him
holding her arms towards him)
more hurtfully than her child-misery
at the earlier parting.

* * * *

Conway has hopes that he will soon be fit
to take a post at Pagnell Grammar School,
where Derrick will be scholar.
He's had a bent towards teaching all along;
Derrick has clinched it. Man's mind to boy's mind,
boy's heart to man's, are bonded. Man and boy
are sure in their relation, each to each,
and each towards Mrs. Delmer, Cherry's babe,
Cherry, and Mrs. Bonner. All, like beads
diverse in shape and colour, share one string
and form a single pattern in the house.
The house itself, unostentatious, square,
solidly built, and homely, seems to breathe
a guarantee that goodness can endure
in spite of death and change.
The stricken widow is serene at last.
Though her speech shuffles, though she drops
    her wool,

she is no longer peevish, exigent,
or prone to weeping. She is glad to watch
from her wheel-chair while Francis and the
boy
are at their lessons.
"That's a good place to stop; put your books by.
I'd like a game of chess till dinner-time.
Would you?" Young Derrick sucks his underlip,
nods an emphatic yes, and brings the board.
They play in silence, Derrick tense to win.
His baby godchild whimpers: Derrick rocks
her cradle, calming her, but silently,
keeping his eyes fixed on the board meanwhile.
The dinner-gong stirs a regretful sigh,
but the familiar pattern of routine,
and stew and currant dumpling, are dear too.
even if chess is dearer. So he clicks
the pieces static on the treasured board;
the game that is begun he yet may win.
He holds the door politely. Francis wheels
the invalid to table. By the fire
a trap-nipped cat is sleeping, swaddle-pawed.
"Be like a full-trained nurse, our Derrick be.
He's stood by Cherry while she's done your foot
and watched just how she done it time on time."
"Maybe he'll be a surgeon when he's grown."
cries Cherry with a smile.
Derrick turns red, for Conway nods assent.
He views the injured cat with swelling love
and has to check an impulse to jump down
and run and stroke her. Mrs. Delmer's face
brightens and dimples. She breaks into song.

"I love little Sooty,
Her coat is so warm,
And if I don't teashe her. . ."

"Derrick sing too?" says Conway. "—You
don't mind?"
Derrick, at meals, is Mrs. Bonner's charge.
"Just while I change the plates and Cherry's gone
to fetch the pudden, if he likes he may."
So Mrs. Delmer starts the verse again.
She hums the seconds, Derrick pipes the air.
Then Derrick marches off to fetch the sauce
and set it carefully in front of Conway.
He spoons his pudding with good appetite,
waits till invited for a second help,
and forms a voiceless thank-you with his lips
that passes muster. Suddenly his ears,
sharper than any of his elders', cock.
He looks a question, scrambles from his chair,
and goes to fetch the letters. There are two;
both are for Conway: one, a mere receipt;
the other Conway pounces on at sight.
All wait, for news of Hulbert. "It's *good* news."
"Ish Hulbert coming?" "No—but Lettice is."
"Good news, good news, for sure! Oh, bless
her heart!"
cries Cherry. "God be thanked," her mother adds
under her breath, while Mrs. Delmer beams
and claps her hands.
Hulbert has scarcely written since the day
he left to meet his sister weeks ago.
Only a few field-postcards trickle in.
No news has come of Lettice.

Conway has sensed disaster of some sort.
Cherry and Mrs. Bonner have been sad,
waiting and watching, praying steadfastly.
Now that good news has come, all three are moved
so deeply that they hardly dare to speak
for fear of baring to the invalid
and to the child depths that they could not gauge
but might be grieved by. Conway schools himself
to speak in level tones that show relief
but less emotion than at heart he feels.
"She has been ill, first in a Nursing Home,
and later at some Convalescent Spa,
getting her strength up. Hulbert will snatch time
for long enough to meet her, so he says,
and see her off from London, but can't come
himself to see us." Tucked in Derrick's cheek
lodge portions of an apple. He chews on,
routine unbroken and the future bright.
Since Francis and the others all rejoice
that Lettice will be coming, so does he.
"Do you remember Lettice, Derrick-boy?"
He shakes his head in silence. "Not at all?"
More headshakes and more chewing. "Her'll
need rest.
Derrick shall take her breakfast on a tray
and set it, careful, on the bedtable."
"You'll like that, Derrick?" Three emphatic nods
signal assent. And now a whimper comes
from Derrick's godchild in the other room.
Cherry runs off, and Derrick's eyes ask leave
to follow. He returns with shawl and stool.
Cherry undoes her bodice. Derrick pulls

the rocking-chair and hearthrug into place.
He sets the stool for Cherry's feet, and spreads
the shawl on Cherry's lap.
He gurgles to his godchild, puts his thumb
into the creases of the tender skin
of her plump neck, then plants a goodbye kiss
into a dimple on her roving hand.
The time has come for him to dry the spoons
that Mrs. Bonner plunges in the suds
beloved by Derrick for their rainbow tints
and pleasant softness. All the good routine
of daily happenings at Foursquare House
is even dearer now to Derrick's heart
than was the good routine at Gospel Oak.
He does not hanker for the china dogs
and willow-pattern dish. Instead he tips
to exact angle the worked fire-screen,
gay with exotic birds,
and taps the hall barometer each day,
moving its surface-pointer with a care
punctilious, as if to be exact
were as important as in surgery.

* * * *

"Ah. . ! Lettice, you look better!" Twenty years
seem lifted from her brother as he stands
and gazes at her. "Yes, and so I am.
I've lived as unborn babes, I think, must live,
hid in that Hydro.
I simply do not understand these months.
I only know my body's taken charge,
forced me to feed it, forced me to sleep sound,
forced me to rest in something not myself.

—Oh, I've not prayed! I've not felt close to God.
I've been a sort of sea-anemone,
sucking in nourishment; a jellyfish,
without a brain or soul, in a rock pool,
aware of nothing but the need to be.
Hulbert, I think the outrage, the assault,
the insolent assault, the *choosing* death,
the pygmy, setting up its will to thwart
something tremendous, something rooted, vast,
the grossness of it . . . Gross, yet frivolous. . .
—oh, am I talking nonsense: I don't know!—
but, anyhow, whatever I had done,
whatever had been done to me—in me,
forced me to *value* life, and cling to it.
—But I had never worked it out like this,
not seen it this way, till I saw your look
of sheer amazement at the change in me."
"Lettice, dear Lettice. . . Thank God for the change!"
"I can't do that. I'm still just flesh and blood,
and bone and nerve and muscle. I'm alive,
but that's the top and tail of what I am.
'Spirit' and 'soul' mean nothing. Even 'brain'
means precious little. I've read nothing good:
just easy novels, women's magazines. . .
I've turned them over idly, then I've drowsed,
wakened to listen for the dinner-bell,
and sauntered to the dining-room to pore
over the menu, hoping the food's good."
"The food at Foursquare House is always good.
There's home-made bread, and fruit, and
new-laid eggs,
for all that there's a war on.

—The war can't last much longer: you know that?"
"If I had got it in me to thank God
how vehemently would I thank Him now!
—Hulbert, can't *you*
come down to Foursquare House?" "Impossible.
I see you off at noon, and then rush back.
When Armistice is signed—there'll still be wounds. . .
But I shall get a holiday some day."
"Perhaps by then I shall have learnt to love.
As Cherry loves: loves Francis. —Hulbert, think!
I've spoken boldly, baldly, of their love.
—But dare I face them? With their baby girl?
Dare I face Mother? Derrick. . . ? Oh, I daren't!
How do I know that when I see them all
something won't stir in me that has not stirred
up in that Hydro, in my hidden pool?
And if it stirs what will that something be?
Will it be love and goodness? Or pure hate?
Oh, it is madness—madness! I daren't go."
"*Some*day you'll have to face them. Face them now.
Go while you're plump and rosy: not so plump
nor yet so rosy as a girl should be—"
"But not a scarecrow: granted. . .
The *secret* hasn't gone, though. Even if
the scarecrow has put on a stone or so,
a tinge of sunburn, a veneer of health,
secrets and sins are there, beneath the skin.
Oh, it is madness—madness!" "You agreed.
You've let me say you're coming: let them hope.
Oh, *how* they want you, Lettice! One and all.
Even young Derrick.
Because the rest are happy, he is too,

to think that you are coming. Francis says
he has no recollection of the time
at Fitzroy Park. It's dropped away. It's sloughed."
"Both Flora Tort and I have dropped away:
two nightmare figures in a past that's dead
Let both remain forgotten." "Lettice, no!
All will be well if you are natural.
Don't delve and probe into his childish thoughts.
Just be yourself."
"But how can I be natural, be myself?
What's nature? What am I?
A jellyfish is natural, is itself,
but I don't feel a jellyfish today.
Since I have seen you, Hulbert, thoughts return.
Feelings are stirring in me. Oh, you're rash!"
"Lettice, the taxi's ordered. It's due now.
Put on your coat and muffler. Take your gloves.
There is a sort of peace at Foursquare House,
a sort of benison, a kindliness.
It's bound to help. Pitch all these fears away. . ."

* * * *

The train slows to a standstill. Passengers
dismount from the next carriage; the door slams.
Soldiers and shoppers trudge or shuffle by.
The train begins to chuff, about to start.
"Please help me with my luggage." Lettice speaks
like someone drugged or dreaming.
"Your bags are labelled Pagnell. This is Pyrte."
The young man is embarrassed, half gets up,
then sits again, repeating "This is Pyrte."
Lettice has turned the handle, pushed the door,
signed to the guard, who lets his green flag fall.

"This is my destination," she affirms
in a flat voice, beginning to get out.
The young man shifts her luggage. He has watched
Lettice grow pale, and paler; watched her write
a postcard. ("A planchette it might have been:
you know, those funny things the mediums use,"
he tells his wife at supper.) "Post this, please:
wherever you are going." "Why not here?
There's a box! Opposite. . ." She leaves the train.
"*You* post it," she says vaguely as she goes.
She does not hear the puzzled man's 'Good-day'.
A porter sees her luggage. "Want a fly?
If so, go on and book one. I've a job,
but when I'm free I'll follow with your bags."
She hands her ticket to the booking-clerk,
and passes on, but finds herself called back.
"Here, Miss! This isn't Pagnell, this is Pyrte."
"I know it isn't Pagnell." "Right ho, then;
I thought you might be making a mistake."
She gets into the fly, but does not speak.
"Where do you want to go?" "To some hotel,
or else some guest-house. Oh," she adds, "but wait.
I've got some luggage coming." "Pyrte's full up.
It's best to book ahead." The man is glum.
The porter shouts across the station-yard:
"Your bags are labelled Pagnell: this is Pyrte."
"I know it is." "I thought you *might* have meant
to go to where they're labelled." He's perplexed.
She tips the porter, heedless what she gives.
The driver grows more civil. "Well, we'll try
the *Silver Lining* guest-house first of all.
But everywhere is shocking short of staff."

Lettice emerges slowly from the state
of tranced compulsion that has come on her
since in her panic she abandoned hope
of finding rest at Pagnell. She must plan;
deal with her situation; be alert.
The fly draws up, and Lettice jumps from it.
Miss Flint, Proprietress, she reads. She rings.
"There *is* a room. . . But I've too much to do.
I can't get maids. They're all on war-time jobs."
"Well, let me lend a hand. I'll dust and sweep.
I'll wash up for you."
"You've got a reference?" "I've been ill for months.
But I'm fit now. I've had to change my plans.
Give me a week to find myself a job.
I'll pay, *and* help you."

* * * *

Upstairs and down, laden with this, with that,
Derrick has bustled self-importantly.
Dahlias and autumn leaves glow near the bed.
The furniture is gleaming.
The rugs have all been beaten, drawers new-lined.
Derrick has made a fretsaw hair-tidy;
he's set the dressing-table glass just right
(he hopes) to mirror the newcomer's face,
fixing it stable with a wedge he's cut.
He pulls in Cherry to inspect and praise.
Cherry herself is all agog with hope,
brushing the baby's hair into a whiff
and pressing smooth the tie-ups for her sleeves,
cutting her toe-nails and her finger-nails,
busy as Derrick; ready, none the less
to hasten when she hears the mistress ring.

She finds her orders hard to carry out
because the shuffling speech describes a dress
laid by since widowhood dictated garb
other than pearl and oyster *crêpe-de-chine.*
At last she tracks it, airs and presses it,
hooks it, admires it, glad to find it fits.
Francis has hobbled round the garden paths
snipping dead roses. In the orchard hang
bright apples that are shouting to be picked.
"Here, Derrick, come and help!
Fetch the chip basket, but before you go
look in the hen-house."
Chatty still cackles over her brown egg.
"Lettice shall have it." Derrick shows it off.
"You're going to take her breakfast to her room,
isn't that right, young man?" Three fervent nods.
"Now get that basket. You will have to wash
in less than half an hour." Derrick's joy
to think how soon it will be time to meet
the London train at Pagnell makes him skip.
A heap of weeds is waiting to be burned.
He takes a running leap and clears it well,
the egg undamaged.
His mood is still one of glad eagerness
at Pagnell station. He and Conway wait
beside the barrier. Conway is keyed up:
excited but afraid. His nervousness
keeps his tongue active.
"Old Porter Bill will bring the bags along.
He knows who's coming. —Mind the posy, boy!
You mustn't squeeze it.
You'll take your cap off, won't you? Make quite sure

she *sees* the posy—sees it's meant for her."
Derrick's agog to give the flowers he's picked.
He clutches Conway's hand and scans the platform.
Soldiers tramp past, and civvies hurry by.
The last has gone.
Old Porter Bill limps up with empty truck.
"Seems as Miss Lettice must have missed the train."
Derrick throws down the posy, spits on it,
tramples it, and then weeps.
"Derrick! My boy! You mustn't mind so much.
We'll find a telegram at home, perhaps.
Perhaps she'll come tomorrow. . ."

* * * *

Again the invalid has rung her bell.
Again her question shuffles. And again.
"Ha' Lettish come?"
And next day when the postcard has arrived:
"Lettish a naughty girl. She only thinks
of pleasing Lettish, not of pleasing me."
Fractious and petulant, the invalid
pushes away her food. Her pretty dress
lies, crumpled, on the floor, where Cherry's grief
has let it lie, neglected as the flowers
in Lettice's rebuffed and silent room.
But Mrs. Bonner takes it off to press,
then moves the slighted flowers, the best towels,
the biscuits, the cold bottles, the clean sheets.
The fretwork hair-tidy she does not move,
for that would serve whenever Lettice came.
Even before the morning post arrived
Cherry felt sure that Lettice would not come,
as she'd not come. Her grief has soured her milk:

the baby can't digest it. Francis reads
the postcard many times, as though, perhaps
some lurking comfort might be found in it.
I'm sorry. Don't expect me. That is all.
Derrick's in sulks. Chatty's brown egg, still whole,
he's shoved aside, with fierce intensity.
Though Mrs. Bonner's eyes are sorrow-filled,
it is with godly sorrow. "Derrick-boy,
be time to fetch the Bible. Leave the egg
if you can't eat it." Derrick's face goes stiff.
It seems he will reject the loved routine.
But suddenly he scrambles from his chair,
settles the Bible in its usual place
in front of Francis, twitches Bonner's sleeve,
gives a confiding smile, then pecks a kiss,
as though to say: 'I'm good again, you see.
We'll still be us, *though* Lettice hasn't come.'
While Francis reads the psalm, his roving thoughts
turn to a waiting chess-board. He *may* win. . .
When morning prayers are over, Francis pats
the wind from Baby. Cherry wipes her eyes,
pours milk for Sooty—Derrick sets it down—
and turns once more to life's familiar ways,
unsoured though chastened, linked to man and babe,
in thankfulness whatever hurt may hap,
whatever ill.

* * * *

Miss Flint has done her single-handed best
to make the *Silver Lining* pay—and please.
Charwomen come; and grumble; come and go;

while in the corners cobwebs come—and stay.
The guests complain, but neither lend a hand
nor leave. 'Where could we go?' they ask themselves.
The week Lettice envisaged when she came
prolongs itself. The idle guests are pleased
to have their beds made for them, their shoes shined,
not uppers only but the bits as well
between the heels and soles.
Lettice smiles wryly when it dawns on her
that she is gaining tips through a technique
derived from Flora Tort.
But, though her smile's sardonic, she shines on.
Noting a boot-lace frayed, she pulls it out,
half caustic and half humbled. Fagged Miss Flint
accepts her unpaid service thankfully
and asks no questions. Lettice has an urge
to work herself so weary that she sleeps
unpricked by guilty thoughts. She makes no friends
among the women boarders: mostly wives
—or mistresses—of men stationed at Pyrte,
who sleep with them when they can get a pass
and take them to the *Falcon* opposite.
They come in fuddled. Lettice has no wish
to join the party at the noisy bar.
The thought of drink revolts her. Not one man
among the score or so who come and go
has power to draw her; but there is a guest
—he rarely speaks to her or to Miss Flint,
he never smiles—who drew her from the first.
She watched him in the crowded coffee-room,
crumbling his bread and staring at a book

propped on the water-jug. One arm hung stiff.
He looked quite young, no older than herself,
younger, perhaps.
"Salad and brawn: all I can do tonight."
His shy acknowledgment conveyed regret
at Miss Flint having household cares—no more.
He turned, about to read. A lettuce leaf
drew his attention from his heavy book;
or, rather, not the lettuce leaf itself
but a small caterpillar on the leaf.
He stared at it, but stared without disgust.
It seemed significant,
though what the thing could signify perplexed
the girl who watched him. Bending down to it,
he let it crawl on to his knuckled fist,
then bore it to the window, raised the sash,
and set it on the windowbox. He sighed:
a sigh that almost was a moan, heaved out
against his will, it seemed. As he walked back
he moved like someone moving in his sleep.
He ate, too, like a person tranced: aware
of nothing but his sorrow-breeding thoughts.
Although he stirs the woman in the girl
he scarcely seems a man, rather a boy,
but a boy broken by a load of grief
almost too heavy for a man to bear.
His grief and his tranced actions bonded them.
Her own tranced actions when she came to Pyrte
were grief-bred actions of a girl in years,
shocked into woman by experience.
Lettice can put no questions to Miss Flint
about this troubled, shy, well-mannered youth.

One day when the two women are alone,
sipping mid-morning tea, with shoes kicked off,
Miss Flint breaks out: "That young chap Fennemore,
he *is* a close one! Never says a word
about himself. There's gossip at the Camp.
Some say the boy hoped once to be ordained.
He served in Flanders; picked up some vile bug;
he still has treatment: goes to Salisbury,
I think to hospital; but that may be
because of his war-wound. He's reading law.
Of course it's only hearsay: I don't *know*.
He looks unhappy." "Desperately, at times,"
says Lettice, needing to control her voice.
"He gets no letters—" Miss Flint checks herself,
for Lettice gets none either.
"He pays his bills like clockwork every week.
I like the fellow. Steady as a rock:
a pleasant contrast to these officers
who seem to change their wives as readily
as he would change his collar. —No more tea?"
"No, thanks. That silver's waiting. *And* the spuds."
He gets no letters. As she rubs the spoons
Lettice contrasts the boy's lack with her own.
She knows that she will get none—never looks;
but every morning when the postman knocks
young Fennemore comes quickly from his room
(his chin still downy) to the letter-rack.
Each morning he goes back, with leaden feet,
an empty-handed beggar, hungry-eyed.

* * * *

Lettice, as housemaid, dusts three photographs
on Fennemore's bed-table day by day.

One shows a grim vast house—a Rectory
it seems, since it is shadowed by a Church.
Another shows a man: like Fennemore,
but older, stronger. In his piercing eyes
is dour severity. His mouth is stern.
He looks a good man, but an austere man.
He wears a cassock. The third photograph
is of a woman vulnerable and frail:
happy, but, Lettice thinks, likely to droop
should trouble test her. Fennemore's straight nose
is like the vulnerable woman's nose;
his chin like hers, his mouth as sensitive,
but sadder, more distressed.
Most of the books are heavy books on law;
but there are poems. Blake's are by the bed.
One day she finds herself impelled to read,
not knowing Blake, and wanting, if she can,
to share the boy's enjoyment.
The page she opens at bewilders her.
It makes her see again, with her mind's eye,
the caterpillar on the lettuce leaf,
and Fennemore, like an automaton,
moving towards the window with his fist
knuckled, and scanned intently.
'*Auguries of Innocence*: what does that mean?
Queer poetry. Why should a cherubim
go silent at the wounding of a lark?
Yet that, perhaps, *is* understandable:
more than the bit about a mother's grief.'

* * * *

Today she must not linger at her work
for she has been delayed by a coarse girl

who came back tipsy when the *Falcon* closed,
and rings, at breakfast time, for aspirin.
Always by ten on every day till now
Lettice has dusted Fennemore's neat room
—he makes his bed himself, then takes his walk.
Today he finds her on her hands and knees,
and steps back, disconcerted.
"I'm sorry if I'm early." "No, I'm late.
I've just on finished." "I say—was it you
who put new laces in my boots? If so,
I owe you for them, don't I?" "Fourpence, then.
I saw that they were fraying, and would break,
and it's so tiresome if you're going out
and haven't any by you." "So it is.
I had some by me actually, but still—"
"I'm sorry. *Stupid* of me. . ." "It was kind."
He gives her fourpence gravely, and they part.
The trivial interchange has stirred them both.
Lettice controls her breathing, but a flush
betrays emotion, and she turns aside
so that she need not meet an officer,
who had a week-end pass to join his wife,
and leaves her sleeping. "Breakfast *any* hour!
It's too bad: blast him!" grumbles fagged Miss Flint
as Lettice joins her (mistress of herself)
to make his coffee.
                    As the weeks go by
Miss Flint depends on Lettice more and more.
She is too shrewd to risk offending her
by seeming quizzy. Though she cannot probe,
she speculates, and watches. '*Some*thing's odd.
Why is she here? She's not a crook, that's plain. . .

She can't have *come* because of Fennemore,
but is it love of him that keeps her here?'
She notices a quickening of breath
when Lettice greets him in the coffee-room
or on the stairs. She sees how Fennemore
—who never showed a gleam of interest
in anyone before—can't keep himself
from looking at her back as she goes out,
though his lids droop as soon as she appears.
She sees that now and then they come from church
together after Sunday evensong.
And Lettice inadvertently one day
reveals that he has told her Bittersby
is where his parson-father is, up north.
Things seem to get no further, though, she thinks.
Young Fennemore looks sad still, and suppressed:
more than he did, indeed, rather than less. . .
Pushing her speculations to one side,
she sweeps the lobby. "T'tch!—That letter, look!
I promised that it shouldn't miss the post,
and now it has." "Not if I run with it,
or, better, take your bicycle. With luck
I'll catch the postman going down the lane."
"Oh, thanks! —For God's sake don't forget
    that brake!
You'll have to walk the hill."
"But then I'd miss the post as like as not."
"Better to miss the post than smash your skull!"

* * * *

Lettice lies at the roadside. She has struck
her head, has wrenched her ankle and her wrist.
She neither sees nor hears, nor knows that blood

is oozing from her temple. Fennemore,
returning from his walk, stops, horrified,
then kneels beside her, helpless, till she stirs.
"You're shaken. Lie relaxed." His hands are tense,
and sweat beads on his forehead. Lettice stares,
then she puts out her hand and gropes for his.
The contact with her hand disturbs his blood.
He pulls his free, in silence. "Speak to me!"
He tries to, but he cannot. "Do you care?
It matters to you that I've hurt myself?"
His breath comes fast and broken. "You do care!
If you can't speak—then kiss me." He bends low,
raises her hand and puts it to his lips,
then drops it, trembling. "You love someone else?"
"No. No one! No one!" "Someone claims you,
    though?
You are committed?" "Nobody claims me!"
"Then, if you're not committed. . . Oh, why? Why?"
He cannot speak. "Is it because you sense
that I've been kissed before, degraded, soiled
by ugly kisses with no love in them?
It makes you draw away?" "No, no, no, *no*!"
Each 'no' that breaks from him seems to hurt more,
but still he holds her off, and is aghast.
"I hadn't seen the man until that night.
He made me drunk. He raped me in my sleep.
I didn't realise—oh, not for months."
She tries to shift. "It hurts, it hurts," she gasps.
"I shouldn't say all this but for the pain.
It seems to make me say it."
She is contorted and convulsed. She gropes
and finds his hand. She clutches it so tight

he couldn't pull it back unless by force.
"There would have been a child. It never breathed.
The doctor took it from me. Horrible. . .
I'd panicked. I'd consented.
You heard about it somehow? You were shocked?"
"I never heard. Of course I never heard.
And 'shocked. . !' " His voice tails off. "*Me*—
    shocked at you?"
Compassion mingles in his tortured face
with all the other strong emotions blent
so hurtfully and inexpressibly.
"Then why, oh why must you hold off? Why? Why?"
The urgency of her bewildered wail
is met by silence. Weakness surges through
her body wracked by pain. She does not hear
the coming of the ambulance, or know
that Fennemore when he had summoned it,
stood at her side convulsed by tearless sobs.

* * * *

"Nothing from Lettice." Others must have seen
the notice in *The Times*. The second post
has brought a dozen letters.
The Church bell tolls, and Rendell Delmer's grave
waits Lois Delmer's coffin. The two men
hold their top hats, smoothed with punctilious care
by Derrick with the pad he loves to use
while Sunday clatters summons from the tower,
joyful and eager, other than the slow
deep plangent single calls that fall today.
Derrick's black tie and arm-band of black cloth
echo his elders mourning. Delmer's needs
leave Cherry scant of time to button up

her bodice and slip on her outer clothes;
but now she joins the others. Hulbert gives
a signal to the undertaker's men.
Martha stands weeping by the basement door.
She is alone, for Mrs. Bonner stays
in the top flat with Delmer. Cherry takes
her place beside her husband, with a sob.
Derrick begins to shuffle after her,
but Hulbert suddenly holds out his hand.
The Conways follow Hulbert and the boy.
Step-son and heir: the precedence is fit.

* * * *

Another post has brought another hurt.
The letters—most of them—bear the address
Miss Delmer. "I dis*like*—it seems all wrong—
reading a letter meant for someone else. . ."
Since Francis finds no comment that could help,
he smokes in silence; yet his presence helps.
"Here's one that's not just condolence. Read this."
Francis grows tense—and tenser as he reads.

> Madam, I take the liberty to send
> my sympathy on reading the sad news
> of your bereavement. Madam, please excuse
> my writing to 'Miss Delmer' if by now
> you are no more Miss Delmer.
> Derrick is on my conscience. I have tried
> the place he came from, and the Waifs and Strays.
> Letters to Gospel Oak get marked 'Not known'.
> I have a husband now. He wants the boy,
> and I do, too. Yours truly, Flora Briggs.

"You'll have to answer this. Let's hope
the boy won't have to leave here." "It's his *home*. . ."
Francis looks whipped. "How *can* we let him go?"

Hulbert, who grieves for Francis, bears no grudge
that Derrick is residuary legatee,
and that the house is now the Conways' house.
The boy is 'brat' no longer. He seems part
with Francis and with Cherry and their child,
with Mrs. Bonner, and old Martha, too,
of a life-pattern comely and complete
that ought not to be shattered. Flesh and blood
link none to Rendell Delmer, yet the whole
seems to be kin to him.
"Derrick's on Flora's conscience?—Get him off!
But she's his mother. *We* can't settle it."

* * * *

Derrick has listened blankly to the news
that Conway stammers. It has been kept back
till Flora's visit is a certainty.
Conway tries hard to discipline his voice.
"They live at Lambeth. They have got a shop.
You'd have a paper-round to do each day.
You'd do that well. I know you'd miss us, boy.
We should miss you. But we should still be friends."
Derrick stares, speechless, at the pendulum
of Dr. Delmer's heavy-ticking clock.
"You'll go and meet them? You will be their host.
Take them to see the Church and the Town Hall.
I think you'll recognise them, and they you.
There won't be many people off the train,
or many schoolboys waiting on their own.
When they have had enough of looking round
bring them on here. The station fly will do.
Their luggage will be safe with Porter Bill;
no need to book it while you're in the town."

Conway drones on. He tries to drug himself
as well as Derrick with his platitudes,
but neither he nor Derrick finds the hurt
alleviated, or the future eased.

* * * *

Briggs wears a loud check suit, a bowler hat,
tan boots, and a bright tie.
Goodwill is beaming from his simple face.
His false teeth do not fit him very well;
they make him dribble. His approaching gait
suggests a barn-dance in its eagerness.
"Ha ha! Ha ha! So here's our little son.
Kiss Mammy, precious! Kiss your Daddy, too."
Derrick stands rigid while his mother pecks.
He ducks aside from Briggs. Briggs gulps his spit,
disheartened. But he soon resumes his croon.
"Why, Mammy, isn't he a handsome lad!
Look at his cap! He took it off so nice.
It's got a pretty picture on it, look!
A shield and lions and some funny words."
Derrick claps on his cap, and pulls his hand
out of the clammy hand of Mr. Briggs.
He stares at Flora. Flora stares at him.
"I'd not have known him. . ."
"He'll have some happy, happy times, my queen,
in dear old Lambeth. Why, he looks too bright
to be a country boy. Doesn't he, Mammy?"
But Mammy interrupts step-daddy's croon.
She packs Briggs off to talk to Porter Bill.
A picture-palace in the Market Place
catches her eye, and soon the three are sunk
in red plush fauteuils, sucking lemonade,

and Briggs is silenced but for hushed bravos,
and oohs of wonder. Bedtime brings release
at last to Derrick. He slips off, unbid.
Briggs whistles through his teeth, eager to please.
His presence paralyses his tense host.
(Plans, arguments, suggestions—all dissolve.)
He snatches respite: halma, drafts, bezique,
old photographs, cat's cradle—anything
to ease poor Flora's tension, and his own.
"I think if you are willing, Mrs. Briggs,
we'll go round to the lawyer for a talk
tomorrow morning. Mr. Briggs, perhaps,
will let his stepson take him for an ice."
Briggs bares his false teeth in a happy smile
and bows his acquiescence zestfully.

* * * *

The lawyer's clerk points Flora to the stairs.
She mounts them, puffing; they are steep, she's stout.
Scanning the lawyer with a wary eye,
she sums him up as 'breezy'. Her jaw drops
—and her eyes fill—to hear the startling news
of Derrick's legacy. She gasps again
to hear that Conway wishes to adopt
the boy: that if she signs some document
he will pass from her, not *be* Derrick Tort,
but Derrick Conway.
"No need to answer now. You'll want a chat
with Derrick's step-dad first. Eh, Mrs. Briggs?"
She clutches her umbrella, swallows hard,
then breaks in sudden speech. "*He'd* better say.
(Not Mr. Briggs, I don't mean Mr. Briggs.)
I've been a rotten mother, all along.

I don't like kids. —And yet I want him home.
I've never had a home, Sir, up till now.
And Mr. Briggs and me, *we* shan't have kids.
I've got too old and fat to take the risk.
(If you'll excuse me.)" Here she bites her lip,
then hurries on. "Briggs truly wants the kid,
he'd *like* to be his daddy. But it's plain
he doesn't take to Mr. Briggs. It's *plain*. . .
I can put up with all his funny ways:
false teeth, and such. (Excuse me. . .)" She goes red.
"But Derrick couldn't. Why, when we were out
he kept on slipping round him to *my* side.
(Not that he's all that keen on *me*, poor kid.)
I didn't know he'd fallen on his feet
or I'd have stayed away. And yet, you see,
I *am* his mother, Sir: there's just a *chance*
that he will choose me. Oh, I *hope* he will!"
She gives a sudden sniff, then blows her nose.
"You'd better put it to him, Sir, not me,
nor Mr. Conway." "Conway, that's O.K.?"
Conway assents. "Let's send him up, Sir. *Now*."
"Right! But he can't just nod; he'll have to speak."
The lawyer grins at Conway, who can find
no smile, or word, in answer.
The lawyer pulls the window up, and waves.
"He's down there waiting for you in the street."
"He's given Briggs the slip, then. Well, I'm blessed!"
When Derrick was sent off with Mr. Briggs
he snatched his bicycle and pedalled—slow,
circling now and again
round his dismayed companion. Thus deterred
from an attempt to take his stepson's hand

in his damp own, poor Briggs toiled—panting—on,
too breathless, too perplexed, for pleasantries.
His Flora finds him with a slopping ice,
neglected. Derrick gulped his lemonade
and made an awkward exit, unexplained
save by a half apologetic squint.
Flora is pained to see her kind man dashed.
She pats his arm, orders a pot of tea,
then settles down to tell her startling tale,
which draws long oohs and ahs of wonderment
and fond distress. Meanwhile she gives Briggs tea
and stirs it for him: all with such an air
of being bonded to him and at one
that soon he is himself again, eyes moist
with adoration of his better half.
Conway has pleaded errands. They're to meet
in twenty minutes in the lawyer's room.
Conway, full early, finds his friend alone.
His eyes demand the news. (He barely doubts
—and yet, she is his mother. . .)
"He says he's Derrick *Tort*, not Derrick Briggs,
nor Derrick Conway; says his father's *dead*;
or, if he isn't dead, he's disappeared.
He hasn't *got* a father. You're his *friend*;
you're *Francis*. And his mother, Mrs. Briggs,
is still his mother. But—she's married Briggs,
and Briggs is not his father.
He wants to live at Foursquare House, and go
to Pagnell Grammar School, until he's big,
and then he wants to go to hospital
and be a surgeon. Oh, he knows his mind!
What's more, his tongue can wag when there's a need.

I'm jolly glad myself he's to be Tort
and neither Briggs nor Conway." Francis sighs.
He stares, abstracted, through his slangy friend,
whose manners he detests, but whom he trusts,
then cries: "There's no *security* this way!
How do we know his mother will not come
and claim him in a year or two?" "Young Tort
—unless I'm much mistook—sees facts *as* facts
more clearly than his would-be father does."
The lawyer winks. He gets two glasses out
and fills them with sloe-gin. "Here, have a drink.
You look as though you need one. —Possibly
that queer young shaver gets his eye for facts
entirely from his dear papa—deceased.
(Or, done-a-bunk.) But I've a kind of hunch
his dear *mama* is shrewd—as well as stout—
and has an eye for facts. She's married Briggs;
and *since* she's married Briggs (and his false teeth)
she's got to let the kid gang his ain gait.
I don't believe she'll claim him." "It's a risk. . ."
"I think the thing will work. You *make* it work!"
He digs him in the ribs and gives a grin.
"She'll keep in touch most like. All to the good.
But she won't claim him. —There's another thing.
(You'll be surprised at this.) He asked me, plump:
'What is a bastard?' 'It's a child', I said,
'born without marriage.' 'Like the pups and calves?'
'Sometimes the very spit of pups and calves.'
He'd thought as much, he said. 'It's not my fault
that I'm a bastard, is it?' 'Good Lord, no!'
'It was my father's fault, my mother's fault.
And bastards mind,' he said, 'because the fault

is someone's they belong to?' 'Sure,' I said.
'And that they mind shows they belong?' says he.
'Too true,' I told him. Then he gave a sigh.
And then he smiled. He clattered down the stairs.
I heard him whistling when he reached the street.
I watched him mount his bike. The dentist's son,
that lad with spots, was coming down the hill.
He put his tongue out as he neared young Tort,
and then—I guessed—he tossed the ugly word.
Tort held an apple that he'd planned to bite.
Instead, he aimed it at young Spotty's neb
and hit it pat. He gave a cheerful whoop
and pedalled on. He's got some spunk, that brat.
—Hullo! Here come the Briggses, arm in arm."

* * * *

The Foursquare household and the Briggses sit
in an uneasy silence. Francis checks
a crazy impulse to put on the clock
and rakes his mind for something fresh to say.
"Derrick—don't go!" he cries out, just too late.
"He knows his mummer's cab be close on due.
He's gone to fetch her summat, I'll be bound,"
soothes Mrs. Bonner. Flora looks relieved.
Briggs sucks his dentures. He has ceased to croon
ebullient praise of everything he sees.
He is perplexed by what has been arranged;
is troubled for his Flora; is aware
that somehow his intentions have misfired.
His Flora takes his clammy hand in hers,
gives it a reassuring squeeze, then spoons
a blob of half-chewed cake from his gay tie.
She does not scold him, does not even frown;

she puts it in her saucer, yet it's clear
from her neat coat, neat hat, neat shoes, neat gloves,
that Flora Briggs has Flora Tort's distaste
for anything disorderly or soiled.
Derrick comes sidling in. He brings a book;
he thrusts it at his mother, takes his pen
from where he proudly wears it at his breast
and lays it on the book. He does not speak.
It is a birthday-book. Flora looks pleased.
She enters 'Flora Briggs', then adds 'née Tort',
and does not pass the book to Mr. Briggs.
"You'll send a card, son, on the twenty-third?
Shall you remember?" Derrick gives two nods.
"*Your* birthday is in April, the fifteenth. . .
What would you like, son? Toffee? Chocolate?
A pair of compasses? Some paints? A book?
Or will you have a photograph of Mum?"
At last he squints a smile. Flora smiles back.
"I'd like a photograph of you, my lad.
Get yourself taken for me—with your cap,
and your school blazer?" Derrick nods three times.
At last the cab is heard, and all stand up.
Derrick waits, silent, holding the door wide.
He does not kiss his mother, but he lets
his mother peck his eyebrow. He avoids
saying goodbye to Briggs; is not rebuked;
waves from the doorstep; heaves a sudden sigh;
clutches his Bonner tightly by the hand;
sobs for an instant; blows his nose and gulps;
taps the barometer; then settles down
to finish *Ivanhoe* (while Sooty purrs,
stroked to complacence) in the windowseat.

"A letter for you, Mr. Fennemore."
Miss Flint would like to see Hugh open it,
but Hugh—convinced the letter is from Lettice,
although the postmark's smudged and until now
he's never seen her writing—disappears.

> Pretend I was light-headed, if you must.
> I wasn't. (And you know it.)
> I've booked a room at Brixwell—Cliff Hotel.
> I go tomorrow. When I've convalesced
> I shan't return to Pyrte. I go for good
> —unless you visit Brixwell.

Horror clutches Hugh, potent as the horror
that clutched at Lettice in the vile consulting room.
Dilemma genders what it did in her
when choice between intolerables seemed to be
forced on her.
Crouching at his bedside, he averts his face
from the pictures on the bed-table.
In a kind of palsy, he abandons hope,
caught in the trap the long-practised sly old Tempter
sets for the victims who lack faith, lack courage,
when nemesis is on them.
His panic precludes reasoning;
it limits him to a daze in which only images come.
These shift, like images seen in a sick man's
nightmare.
He endures torment, banned by his panicking
from God-trust, God-hope, any slightest stir of
God-seeking;
barred, by his fear, from abandonment
to Hands that wait to grasp him.

He sees cold scorn flicker in the eyes of one who
once loved him.
With a ghastly shift of face his father becomes
Lettice,
and *his* outrage, *his* disgust,
her disgust, *her* outrage.
Lettice's eyes flash scorn that horrifies him.
Flinching from Lettice's taunts,
he utterly lacks hope.
Then different visions, no less dreadful, torture him.
First his mother, stricken by wounding compassion,
surveys him silently with hurt brimmed eyes;
then hurt brimmed eyes gaze at him from his
lover's face,
gone haggard, pinched by grief.
Another vision comes:
baffled unhappiness at pushed-off love,
gendered by seeming coldness, callously proffered.
The horned dilemma menaces:
confession one horn, silence the other.
Each horn in turn abrades him.
Muffled groans rack him.
But at last as he crouches, not reasoning, not praying,
he finds his own groaning merge with supernal
groaning.
He is too dazed, too confused, to guess
that Lettice has had contact,
brief but potent,
with One she thought never to have contact
with again.
Her small whiff of prayer, winged like a bit of
thistledown,

has flitted up, and met the Interceder-hurricane,
deflecting it towards him.
Groanings unutterable persist, human mingled
with supernal:
groanings that end in action.
The endurer is no longer merely an endurer.
He takes his pen and writes, stricken still
but paralysed no longer.

* * * *

Lettice is staring at the jesting nurse
who trips this way and that. The post has come.
The nurse distributes cards with garish views,
packets, or welcomed parcels. Now and then
she muddles things, omits, bestows amiss,
is summoned to retrieve a vulgar card
left with a prudish patient,
who stirs derisive glances by her snort.
At last! A single letter in her hand,
the nurse approaches Lettice. Lettice gasps,
deaf to the nurse's jests, blind to all else
but Fennemore's contorted hand-writing.

> Lettice, I'll come.
> But don't, *don't*, let your nearness torture me.
> Let me hold off from you. *Make* me hold off.
> You weren't light-headed; oh, I know you
> weren't!
> We won't pretend. But there has *got* to be
> a fence between us. Now—perhaps for months,
> and that because I've sinned.
> It tears me to write this; it will tear you.
> Tell me to stay away if that seems best.
> Tell me

The twisted writing breaks off short

without a signature. She reads but once.
She doesn't waver, doesn't even *try*
to plumb Hugh's torment: knows he must not pass
out of her life to silence. *How* he's sinned
seems to her utterly irrelevant.
She scrawls a single word, on a torn sheet,
then thrusts the paper in an envelope,
addresses it, and hurries to the post,
brushing aside a nurse who questions her.

* * * *

The sea dunts harshly at the Brixwell cliffs.
Curlews and gulls are crying and the wind
spatters tossed foam on Lettice and on Hugh.
Neither hears gulls or sea-break; neither feels
the salty foam accost them.
"It doesn't *matter*!" Lettice pushes back
the hair that blows across her mouth and eyes.
"We both are sinners: *my* sin doesn't make
me someone to be shrunk from! Hugh, we're bound,
bound quite irrevocably! You *know* we are.
Why, when I blurted out what *I* had done
you felt—compassion. *Did* you feel contempt?
Did you feel scorn or loathing? Why should I?
Oh, I don't ask for details! I don't *want*
to probe and penetrate. There is no need.
Nothing could turn my love into disgust.
Nothing could cut you off. Why, I belong
to you, and you to me. You always will.
Now, and in eternity, we're one.
You're trembling, but you know that it's the
truth."
Hugh trembles and grows paler. He shrinks back

when Lettice flings her hands to catch at his.
Her fierce intensity and confidence
leave him dumbfounded. Never has speech come
with such strong spate of sureness to his lips
as speech has come to Lettice.
He finds no words to voice his panic dread
that, since her sureness stems from innocence,
to wither innocence would wither love,
or, if not wither love, would utterly
break down the lover.
His father's letter stabs, as it stabbed first
in Flanders and impelled him to the brink
of suicide.

> Your Mother's innocence had shielded her
> from knowing there could *be* such wickedness.
> Don't write. Don't come. She's broken by your
>   news.
> I shall not write again.

He's still in Flanders: back in the dark Church
where, desperate, he struggled for the thread,
the fragile thread, of faith, that drew him back
from the near brink. His lover stares at him.
She sees his fingers groping, unaware,
to grip the little cheap medallion
that dangles from his watch-chain; and, to her,
he seems like a small boy on his first day
at his first school, who keeps back his hot tears
by clinging to some trinket brought from home
to give him comfort. The unconscious act
stirs a protective pity in her heart
more suited to a mother for her child

than a girl-lover needing to be wooed.
Impulsively she grasps, then strokes, his hand,
caressing it with a strong tenderness,
as though he were the woman, she the man.
He forces speech; he falters. Every word
and every gesture he has had to bear
scalds and appals him. "I was wrong to come.
You shouldn't have said come. Don't fondle me.
I must go back to Pyrte.
I may seem like a shrinking girl to you,
or a small boy. I may seem infantile.
But I'm a man, and mustn't be a man.
You torture me. I said don't torture me:
don't let your body tempt me. But you do."
A sound that's half a sob and half a laugh
breaks from his lover.
"Why, there's no train to Pyrte! The last has gone.
Oh, Hugh, I'm not a temptress! But I can't,
I simply can't pretend that we don't love
when I'm so sure—so certain, that we do.
Why should a sham possess us? Truth *is* truth,
and to deny it must bring misery.
Why should sin be a barrier to you
when it is not a barrier to me?
It need not be a barrier to you."
Hugh strains himself upright. He schools himself
to speak as he has never spoken yet.
Neither a girl's nor child's his bearing now.
"Go back to the hotel. I shall stay here.
I've got to be alone. I've got to think.
Later, we'll talk, at dinner; not like this
but as most people talk, as *lovers* talk,

when they're observed. With reticence, not false,
but decent. After I have thought, have prayed,
after we've dined in public, I've a hope
I'll make *my* firm conviction master yours.
Perhaps I'll make you trust me. Go and change.
And when you change your garments change your
    mood.
Your mood: I don't say self. Be yourself still.
but be the self you're meant to be. Now go.
I order you to go." She flings away,
still unconvinced, still certain she is right,
but too astonished to renew her plea.
A dozen times she's tried to interrupt:
has broken out in protest.
Each time he has rebuffed her, silenced her.
The hand he's raised has trembled, yet the words
its gesture checked *were* silenced.
She marvels. As she changes, her thoughts swirl.
Hugh Fennemore is still Hugh Fennemore;
she recognises that: still vulnerable,
still a bewildered boy, with downy chin
—it's always smooth or downy; though he shaves
it never bristles—; but, though vulnerable
and pitifully young, yet with a hint
of dignity and power unguessed till now.
She finds the coffee-room. Hugh waits for her.
A couple share their table, middle-aged,
well-groomed and civil. Lettice is surprised
to find chat flow. They talk of anagrams,
the weather-forecast, and the difference
between a well-cooked plaice and well-cooked dab.
Whist follows, after coffee. Then the wife

sings in a pretty tinkling gentle voice.
The hotel clock strikes midnight, stridently.
All other guests went off to bed betimes,
and now the wife and husband follow them.
The embers in the log fire glow and pulse,
deaden, and glow again, then fall to ash.
Hugh turns to Lettice. Though his lips are white
and his hands tremble, he is resolute.
"Give me three months. In three months I shall know
whether I dare come back. Three months apart.
We may be bound for ever. But tonight
—tonight, tomorrow, and for weeks to come,
we've *got* to stay apart." "Hugh, why? Why? Why?
We *know* we're bound for ever. Oh, we'll wait,
of course we'll wait, until the banns are read,
or licence granted. I'm not—*wanton*, Hugh.
But, to be cut apart, to cut ourselves
apart, by our own will, for three whole months:
it's folly! There's no need: how can there be?
No! Let's tell everyone that we're engaged;
let's live as other men and women live
who mean to marry. Let's kiss. Let's hold hands.
Oh, why must we be parted? Hugh, it's mad!
It isn't *natural* when lovers love
to hold themselves apart—so stiff and scared.
Let us be natural." She sees again
the little badly taken photograph
of Cherry on the swing, her face turned up
to Francis: gay and blissful, both of them,
as innocent and glad as animals
and yet with something God-like in them too;
and as she sees she knows that jealousy

has dropped from her as utterly as leaves
pushed by a new year's growth will drop from boughs
that rustled all through winter, jaundice-sere.
"Oh, Hugh, come home! I want to show you off.
I want to tell my mother: brag of you.
I want to tell my brother, and my friends.
I haven't seen them—oh, for far too long!
I've treated them disgracefully. Come home.
They will forgive. . .
There is a boy, a little boy I wronged:
you would be 'Uncle Hugh' to him and I
would be his 'Aunty Letty'—" " 'Brag' of me. . .
Oh, Lettice, stop! You torture me. This talk
of being 'natural'. . . You've *got* to stop."
"Take me up north: to Bittersby. *Your* home."
She hurls the words that torture Fennemore
as though some demon urged her.
"I want to see that old grey Rectory.
I want to know your parson-father, Hugh.
I want to know your mother—hear them say:
'So this is Lettice'; see them look at me
not only as the girl their son brings home
but as the future mother of his child.
—Don't stand there looking tragic! There's no sin
God can't or won't forgive. Oh, Hugh, Hugh, Hugh,
my love for you has brought me back to God!
We are on speaking terms again at last.
I never thought I'd turn to Him again,
or hear Him whisper, as I have of late,
since I've known you, since I've learnt how to love
someone who's not myself. —Why, all these years
I've loved myself and nobody at all

except myself. My father sometimes, though?
Yes, and perhaps my brother. But far less
than that complacent pygmy, that smug wretch,
whom love of you is able to transform
into a different person. Don't you *see*
that God has sent me to you?
Who made me suddenly get out at Pyrte,
when I got scared of Pagnell, if not God?
I was a coward—and I broke my word. . .
But it was *God* who said: 'Get out at *Pyrte*,
now you've determined that you won't go home'."
Her strong emotions silence her at last.
Her breath is stifled.
She stretches out her arms to Hugh and cries.
Though Hugh has prayed for strength to conquer
strength,
he has not prayed for strength to combat tears.
His arms receive her; his defence is down.
She cannot check her weeping. He is torn
by love, by pity, by bewilderment.
He almost carries her upstairs to bed,
leaves her, still crying, in her lonely room,
and shuts himself in his.
Desire consumes him, pity is a flame
that scintillates and kindles, as a fire
glows and advances, wind-blown, through the furze
when frost has crisped it.
At length, hardly aware of what he does,
and with no vile intent, no brutal urge,
but dizzied by his pity and her grief,
he goes to her.
She claims caresses, sure that they are meet

for solace in her weakness, like a child
who yearns for comfort in a baffling hurt.
The contact of their bodies seems to prove
that joy not separation is their due.
She strengthens contact, not in stirred desire,
but certain that her judgment and not his
derives securely from the Paraclete.
She grasps conviction as her mother Eve
grasped the sweet globe in Eden, unaware
that in her arrogance she beckons on
the Angel with the flaming sword to swoop
and drive them from the Garden. She is blind
to all but what seems wisdom, seems divine,
in her bold grasp of the forbidden fruit.
And she weeps still, not *seeming* arrogant.
Had she seemed arrogant he might have found
strength to command her, as he did before.
Had she attempted to stir up desire
by any expertise in wantonness,
rather than yield he would have struck her face.
The wileless innocence of each caress
is his undoing.
Had not her mother's fondness intervened,
(foiling her father's perspicacity)
forewarned, she would have glimpsed danger ahead
and have escaped it.
But for that nightmare night, integrity
(carnal integrity, mere virginhood,
unconscious) might have saved her.
Now, violated and yet ignorant,
she fondles, clings to him, a needy child,
still crying, unaware that she has stirred

his passion past his bearing. Frenzy comes,
a blinding frenzy, a delirium.
The now annihilates the heavy past,
the heavier future.
Adam to Eve is victim, as to the Worm
Eve has been victim, through the subtilty
that makes her arrogance seem confidence
in divine will and purpose.
Eve trembles to her Adam, yields herself
in dazed astonishment, then struggles free,
too late to spare disaster.
For him the now dissolves in ignominy
while past and future, pitiless as blocks
that crush a man between them on the rack,
stifle and agonise him. Misery—
cowed misery, calamitous and base—
possesses him, engendering despair.
She—motionless,
mazed beyond speech or reason, blind and deaf
to past and future—lies anaesthetized.
The now is all, exhaustion all. Her will
succumbs to dreamless sleep: sleep too profound
for any sounds to seem significant.
But there are sounds, faint sounds, from the
    next room,
where he, like someone moving in a trance,
empties the bedroom drawer and packs his bag,
takes from his purse with numb bewildered hands
a sovereign to cover his account.
He puts it in his bedside candlestick,
then adds a florin for the chambermaid.
Each stealthy movement has its origin

in panic terror even more extreme
than that which in the vile consulting-room
hypnotised her to choice of death within.
No fragile thread of faith restrains him now.
He lets the subtle Tempter's guiding hand
direct his footsteps to the sea-dashed brink.
Not till the waters close above his head
does any plea for mercy stir in him.

* * * *

Lettice sits huddled in the London train.
'My well-beloved has left me: why, why, why?'
The pounding of the engine pounds the words
into her battered being. 'Why, why, why?
I have *more* need, not less; *he* has more need.
We are bound closer—closer.
Why three cold months of bruised bewilderment
before he comes to claim me? Why, why, why?'
Four restless days, four restless nights, have passed
since his desertion. On her lap there lies
a *Morning Post*. She means to search for jobs;
as yet she's too collapsed.
Her fellow travellers are officers:
two scan their morning papers, silently;
the third is dozing. Suddenly one speaks,
and with his opened copy of *The Times*
taps his slumped neighbour. "Good Lord, man,
    read this!"
He points the place. "It's that young Fennemore.
I'm sure his Christian name was Hugh—the chap
who'd hoped to be ordained."
The paragraph is read, and read again.

"*Could* it have been an accident?" "It *could*. . .
The coroner will have to settle that.
It doesn't look much like an accident."
"He took his illness far too much to heart."
"I heard he did."
"His parson father was to blame for that.
The boy knew nothing: joined up straight from
school,
full up with moonshine." "Didn't he get hit?"
"Yes, shrapnel in the elbow. That was how
it came out he had got the other thing."
"His people took it badly?"
"That parson father was a heartless chap:
told him the shame had got his mother down,
and it might end her.
Told him he mustn't write; mustn't go home.
The poor fool brooded on it."
Lettice has sat immobile. Now she sags,
her pallor such that it can't be ignored.
"Best get your head between your knees." She fails.
One of the men has got a flask. "Drink this."
But she can't drink it. All her world goes black.
At Paddington she sways, then faints again;
comes to to find a police-woman in charge.
She pulls herself together, books a bed,
and spends a night of fevered agony.
In her delirium a tremendous hand
sponges the recent past from consciousness.
Against a slaty background smudged and vague
faces come clear, then shift, while voices rise
and fall to silence.
The young man in the train, the booking-clerk,

the porter, stare at her, as one by one
each mouths the same words, not a hundred times
and not a thousand, but ten thousand times
in hideous succession. This is Pyrte.
Your bags are labelled Pagnell. This is Pyrte.
(This is my destination.) This is Pyrte.
Your bags are labelled Pagnell. This is Pyrte.
(This is my destination.) Then a voice,
which is her own voice, dunts in someone's ear
(in whose she can't remember): It was God
who said get out at Pyrte, get out at Pyrte,
since you won't go to Pagnell, go to Pyrte.
God made me suddenly get out at Pyrte.
My destination is my destiny. . . .
Next day she roams till dark, still blank to all
that intervenes, for when a glimmer lights
the slaty background, swift the hand again
moves the great sponge. At night, drugged by fatigue.
she sleeps the clock round: waking, feels dazed need
of nourishment. It is too late to ask
for breakfast, so she finds an A.B.C.
and having eaten there she notices
a card announcing vacancies in staff.
It dawns on her that she had come to town
to look for work. (Again the moving hand
obliterates a something on the slate
that seemed about to form.)
She's taken on as washer-up, below.
The work is hard: she goes to bed at night
so weary that again she sleeps like one
drugged, until morning.
She faints at work three times within two weeks;

is sacked, though not unkindly.
She comes aware of bodily distress
that brings to mind
—again the hand, again the sponge—the talk
of her coarse colleague at the orphanage,
till then not thought of. In a squalid street
she notes a doctor's plate, his surgery hours.
She waits her turn as frigid as a stone.
She struts into the surgery, chin up,
thrusting all weakness from her.
She tells her hateful symptoms in a voice
that is not Lettice Delmer's but a girl's
loud and discourteous and cynical:
and when she leaves she still is hard and bold,
in all her seeming, even to herself:
as shameless as a woman of the streets.
The cheap hotel receives her for the night:
tomorrow she will settle up and leave.

* * * *

Church bells are clashing wildly.
Excited singing breaks from group to group.
Giant confetti hovers in the air;
from every office window it is tossed:
papers and forms discarded with delight,
those that the Armistice has rendered null,
and many that it has not: who's to care?
They flutter to the heads of men and girls
who link their arms and sway, laughing and sobbing.
Strangers accost each other, strangers kiss.
A stranger sways towards Lettice,
then ducks aside, rebuffed and almost scared,
for Lettice wears the pall of a fierce gloom.

The tumbling glory of the wild-rung bells
beats, mocking, on her ears.
She lets the devil have his way with her,
repeats his comments on the hymn that swells
out of the open Church, thronged to the doors;
echoes his vile derision,
permits his caustic venom to possess
her spirit and contort her bitten lips.
She turns her back on Holy Trinity,
passes the garish portals of the Stoll,
and makes her way into the crooked street
that lies behind it.

Blatant clangs the bell,
crude as the diseases that gaol the patients
in the Special Hospital.
The porter is pushing some trolley laden with soiled
    dressings,
or stoking some furnace in some remote cellar.
He pays but scant heed to the rollicking Church bells
or to the hysterical yells and singing of the patients.
To the harsh clangour of the bell above the portico
he will attend at his convenience.
At length he bulls his way, snorting, across the yard
and grudgingly gives entrance.
Lettice, wearing the Devil's shield and buckler,
throws up her chin and follows.
She twirls the doctor's chit as though it were a
    guerdon
that brought honour with it.
She almost swaggers:

past the trolley laden with metal containers of
loathsome burnables,
up harsh cold steps,
along harsh cold corridors
to the door of Matron's office,
marked: *Private. Knock and wait.*
The porter knocks and waits,
giving at intervals his bull-like snort.
Patients shuffle by from treatment.
Some, as they pass the porter, mouth a greeting
or a curse.
Two brave the notice *Silence in the Corridors*
and yell "War's over!", dancing a fox-trot with
abandon.
The painted walls, bile-green with ox-blood dado,
scab and flake above the hot water-pipes.
A catch, released by Matron, opens the door at last.
With a nod that curtly bids her sit,
Matron takes the paper that Lettice boldly proffers.
"You're Mara Stone?" "That's right." "Say 'That's
right, Matron' ".
" 'That's right, Matron'." Mara's voice mimics
Matron's.
"You will gain nothing here by insolence.
—Of no fixed abode?" " 'That's right, Matron'."
Again the mimicked voice. Matron's look meets
Mara's.
Mara will not flinch. She outstares Matron.
"The first thing you will do here is to wash that face.
Make-up's forbidden. I will see you later
as to treatment."
Matron pings her bell. She writes in triplicate

the details from the doctor's paper.
"Follow the nurse. She will instruct you
as to our regulations."
Again the mimicked voice: "Oh, *thank* you, Matron."

* * * *

Thoughts tangle Hulbert nightly, barbed as the wire
that's tortured many of the wretched men
he tries to heal.
He feels a kind of gangrene of the soul;
and he can neither drain nor amputate.
With Christmas near he drafts a nameless plea
and sends it to *The Times* and *Morning Post*.

> A sea-anemone? A jellyfish?
> Reveal the Hydro and relieve our fears.
> Brother, and boy, and friends, we all nurse hopes
> that you will make our Christmas less forlorn.

But Lettice does not see *The Morning Post*,
nor yet *The Times*.
His tortured ingenuity is vain.

* * * *

Lettice has shed her braggadocio.
She is in tears: in name is Mara Stone
but not in essence. Like a flower whose stem
is plunged in scalding water, she has drooped,
for memory has come back: the erasing hand
no longer wields its sponge.
The door clicks open at her feeble knock.
"Sit down, child. What's the matter? Here, sniff this."
The Matron's smelling-salts are powerful:
a shudder runs through Lettice; she can speak.
"I've come for my discharge, please Matron. Now."

Her bearing has no insolence today.
"You're foolish, Mara. Stick it out. Be brave.
Where can you go? You're still infectious, child."
"I will infect nobody. Matron, please. . .
I know my destination." "Girl, you're mad.
Stay here until you're cured. You're nearly cured."
But Lettice shakes her head. "My discharge, please."
The Devil feels no need to arm her now
with braggadocio and insolence.
He deems her his, exempt from all assault
by Michael and his cohorts.
Her pride's dispensable since it's replaced
by something yet more congruous with his aims.
He murmurs his directions in her ear.
Like sewer rats they creep towards his home,
while Mrs. Bonner prays, with eyes tight shut,
"Deliver her from evil. Keep her safe."

* * * *

As Helen Cordell, heedless of the lift,
runs down the office stairs two at a time,
she means to make her way into the Strand
to buy some Christmas presents: baby-clothes,
and gewgaws to cheer up down-hearted friends.
Now and again she needs to cross the road
and take the crooked street behind the Stoll.
Today she has no cause, yet crosses Kingsway.
She scolds herself for foolishness, yet scolds
good-temperedly. An impulse in the past,
not once nor twice, seeming as crazed as this,
deflecting from some ploy planned well ahead,
has revealed later such deep pertinence
that she is loath simply to say 'You fool!'

and do her shopping.
The litter-box clamped to the iron rail
that she has passed a dozen times a year,
for many years, without a glance or thought
today stirs up a flitting memory:
a daphne spray, revivable though crushed,
tucked in the belt of a crisp-laundered frock,
one April that seemed June before the war.
December now. The imaged daphne spray
yields place to a compulsive present fact,
for Lettice moves, like a sleep-walker, on,
too tranced to notice Helen. Helen turns
and follows close, marking how Lettice creeps
as one whose destination is prescribed
irrevocably, one whose steps are forced
by something more insistent than her will,
some dreadful gravitation, not of earth
but of a centre hellishly malign,
the sluggish Thames conniving.
Men stare and women stare. Lettice is blind
to wonder and to pity.
Her dragging feet find desperate energy
and break into a run so wildly swift
that Helen has not grasped her.
One instant, silhouetted against cloud,
she stands and sways, then dives. Confusion now
as men and women form a seething clot
to crane and splutter.
"Throw out that life-belt!" It is Helen's cry.
"She's gripped it." "She's let go again." "She's sunk."
"No, can't you see she's risen?" "Sunk again."

"Look, there's a boat." "It's almost there." "She'll
drown.
Oh, what possessed her?" "Sinking—the third time."
"The boathook's caught her." "A-a-h, they'll save
her yet."
"Well done: they've got her." "Ring the police." "No,
don't:
I'll be responsible. Leave things to me."
Heads turn, like one, to see who gave the cry,
and then, like one, turn back.
"A job to get her up those slimy steps:
dead weight and all." "I'll bet she isn't dead."
"She moved her foot." "She's breathing." "She's
not drowned."
"If she's not *drowned*, she'll catch her death of cold."
"Who'll lend a coat?" cries Helen. "A thick coat!"
"It's luck as it's a muggy day: no wind."
"She'll need an ambulance to hospital."
"That taxi—stop it!" (Helen's voice again.)
"Thanks for the coat: I'll see you get it—dried.
What's your address? Here, use this envelope."
"That taxi wouldn't stop." "Then try another!
Wait, offer him this sovereign—for his tip."
The second driver doesn't shirk the job.
He sees the dripping woman, knows time spent
in drying out his car will lose him cash,
but, decent-hearted, only wants his fare.
Women screen Lettice, strip her clumsily,
huddle her in the borrowed overcoat,
wring out her dripping clothes as best they can,
then heap them, sodden, on the taxi floor.
A man half heaves, half shoves her. Helen helps;

she's got in first, to pull. Then, leaning out,
"Great Russell Mansions, facing the Museum:
the second block," she cries. "And thank you,
    friends."
They're off. A policeman comes. "Here, what's all
    this?"
Only the driver took in the address,
and no one thought to note the number plate.
The policeman listens, grunts, and goes his way.

* * * *

"That you, Jim?—I am *sorry*. I can't come.
Of course you're disappointed! I am too.
I'll come for Easter. Love to Jessica.
There's someone needing me. I can't explain.
I must get back to her." Helen rings off.
Lettice is drowsing fitfully. She moans.
Hot bath, hot towels, hot tea, and blazing fire
have made her shudder less.
She has not spoken. Helen chafes her hands,
then slides beef essence in between her lips.
"There's just a chance she'll live," the doctor says.
"Keep her well propped. She's sure to slip. So watch,
and haul her up. The pulse is poor," she adds,
"but a bit steadier than it was at first.
—Helen, are you a saint? Or just a fool?"
"Oh, just a fool. —When will you come again?"
"I'll look in before bedtime. Don't you move;
I'll let myself out."
Helen sits watching, serving when there's need.
She keeps herself awake with *Sherlock Holmes*.
She reads no scriptures and she says no prayers.

* * * *

For Hulbert Christmas merely is forlorn.
But for the rest—though Lettice stays away,
though only Mrs. Delmer's wraith is there
to sing 'O little town of Bethlehem'
(slurring her s's but in perfect tune)
—Christmas is Christmas still.
Delmer's too young to know what Christmas is,
and yet she seems to sense a festival.
She stares and gurgles, kicks her sturdy legs,
and shakes her rattle.
Boxing-day comes. Hulbert need strain no more
to hide his gloom. And yet it hurts to go. . .
Derrick is leaving with him. He'll be met
at Paddington by Flora. Not by Briggs,
for Briggs has maiden sisters who have claimed
a brother's help in drawing up their wills.
He's roped in his old partner, now retired,
to carry on the business for a week.
Flora has planned to take her son about,
show him the sights of London, do him proud,
and Derrick is excited: so much so
that had not Hulbert touched him on the arm
he would have left behind him in the train
the envelope that Hulbert has addressed
and shyly proffered.
"I don't get many letters out in France.
I'd like to hear about your doings, boy."

* * * *

"Well, son, you'll have to settle what we do.
There's that Museum where the mummies are,
and all those books—thousands, so I've been told,

all in a circle, under a big dome.
I was in service with an author once—"
(Flora stops short, then brushes from her mind
the clever gentleman, the scientist,
whose commerce with his handsome parlourmaid
had not been limited to talk of books
—or mummies.
She cannot speak of him to anyone,
and least of all to Derrick, whose chin's cleft
repeats the chin's cleft of that gentleman.
She hurries on to talk of something else,
and with her flush her recollections fade;
she is herself again. A banished past
must not disturb the present.)
"Or, we could hire a boat in Regent's Park.
It's warm enough: I never knew such weather.
—Well, which is it to be, son? Back you go
to Wilts tomorrow, so you can't have both."
Derrick, torn two ways, views them thoughtfully.
The mummies would impress the Pagnell boys. . .
To take his mother in a rowing boat,
and show her the right way to ship your oars. . .
"Well, which is it to be? Are you asleep?"
Flora won't let him shake his head or nod;
he has to use his tongue when he's with her.
"Mummies," he says. "Then mummies it shall be!"
She hails a cab, contented with his choice:
she is too portly to enjoy a boat.
The air is mild as autumn; sunshine warms
the portico where basking trippers rest
after they've traipsed round the galleries
and bought their postcards.

Not all are trippers; there are two whose steps
have been but few—and slow. The golden day
has tempted Helen to persuade her guest
to totter out. She has not stirred till now
beyond the bedroom.
"Why—Miss *Lettice*! *Well*!
(Miss Delmer, I should say.) What a surprise!
—But aren't you looking ill. . ." "It's someone else
you thought you recognised. I'm Mara Stone."
"I beg your pardon, Madam. My mistake.
Come Derrick. Don't stand staring. Don't be rude."
Derrick pays little heed to all the books.
He views the mummies with a listless eye.
When he gets back to Lambeth he is sick.
"It's the rich food," says Flora. "You're not used
to what they give you in these restaurants.
Let's hope you perk up by tomorrow, son."
Derrick creeps into bed, is sick again,
and has to call his mother. When she's free
she does not find herself a ploy, but sits
and stares into the fire. '*Was* it her?
I'm Mara Stone, says she. . .
She's got a right to keep her secrets close.
—*Ought* I to tell her brother? Well, I won't. . .
That woman with her: I've seen her before?
She used to visit at the hospital:
that's where I've seen her! *Christ*! Oh, *what* a go. . .
The boy—I bet he saw as 'Mara Stone' . . .
well—*was*n't Mara Stone. Now, will he blab?
Not him. He's such an oyster. Things must slide.
It might upset him if I warned him off. . .'

*   *   *   *

Lettice has had a night's rest since her walk.
She fainted as she crossed Great Russell Street.
Some passers-by helped Helen haul her up,
half drag, half carry her to the flat-lift.
Since then she has not spoken of the chance
that showed she has another name than 'Stone'.
What talk there's been has been of malted milk,
the winter sunshine, Helen's placid cat. . .
Her guest's identity, the suicide
that she attempted, where she goes to next,
the hostess seems contented to let be,
not in indifference, nor with conscious tact,
but with a patience natural as a bud's,
waiting to be a blossom.
Helen has made no joke since Lettice came,
nothing so solid as the lightest joke,
and yet there is a ripple when she speaks,
a glint like sunlight on a breeze-stirred pool,
suggestive of a dancing happiness,
a gaiety within her, not suppressed,
but waiting to be blown like thistledown
when the wind rises. Laughter waits the wind,
compassion waits no wafting. Lettice stirs,
summons what vigour she has left in her,
scans Helen and leans forward from her chair
so that her feeble voice may not fall short.
"*Why* did you save me?" "I don't really know.
I didn't stop to think it out at all."
"You did it for the Christ outside my soul
—or for the Christ within?" "Why, Christ and
I. . .
We've not been introduced."

"Whom had you meant to spend your Christmas
with?"
"With friends. Up north." Lettice sinks back. She
broods.
"I'd hoped to understand. I see I can't.
—But aren't there questions you must put to me?"
"No, I don't think so. Tell me, if you like.
But there's no need."
"I am infectious. Shameful. Through my fault.
I shouldn't be here." "When I saw you first
you were just coming from the hospital . . ."
"You followed all that way? —You must have done.
What made you do it?" "You looked all to bits.
I was afraid you'd try to take your life."
"Have you rung Matron?" "Yes." "She wants me
back?"
"It's up to you. She'd help." "You told my name?"
"Of course I didn't! It was only chance
I knew myself. How *could* I pass it on?"
"You visit at the hospital?" "At times."
"You've known it for some years?" "For six or
seven."
"You knew my father?" "Yes. I knew him well.
He spoke about your mother—and you too.
I saw your mother once." "You always knew
I wasn't Mara Stone?" "I didn't *know*."
"You guessed I was his daughter?" "No! I thought
your voice reminded me of *some*body."
"You'll have to take me back. Don't be afraid. . ."
"You'll never—dive again?"
"No; something happened. When I dived before
I thought that I should join a friend—in Hell."

"Would Hell be Hell if you could join a friend?"
"I know I *shouldn't* join him if I dived.
That's what I've learnt. There isn't much I know,
but that I'm sure of."

* * * *

Derrick has *Chums* and *Comic Cuts* and *Chimps*.
Flora has packed them with his sandwiches.
He neither reads his comics nor unpacks
his generous lunch-box, only gnaws his thumb:
a trick he has not yielded to for years.
At last he writes a letter.
The words come quickly; he has formed each phrase
before he touched his paper and his pen.
He dots an *i* and puts a comma in,
then reads the letter through a second time.

> Dear Mr. Hulbert, yesterday we saw
> Miss Lettice. Mum thought she looked very ill.
> She said her name was Mara Stone. She said
> she wasn't Lettice Delmer. But she was.
> I saw her scar. I wish I never threw
> that bottle at her.
> We went to see the mummies. I don't think
> *she* come to see the mummies. It was warm.
> I think she might have come to feel the sun.

He puts his letter in the envelope
addressed to Captain Delmer.
When the train stops he sees a letter-box;
quick, posts his letter; jumps back to his place
and eats his sandwiches. He didn't know
till he began how much he needed them.
Chums, *Chimps*, and *Comic Cuts*, he leaves unread.

Delmer is teething. Cherry soothes in vain.
"Oh, shut your mouth, you little misery,
or put a sock in it. . ." "*Derrick*! My boy!
—You'd better go to bed: you're tired out.
We'll come to say goodnight. —Don't slam the door!"
But Derrick slams it.
"What *can* have happened? *Delmer* on his nerves!"
" 'Twere best to let him get himself to bed,
and then I'll coax him." "He'll be that upset
when once he is himself again, poor lad,"
sighs Cherry, rocking Delmer on her knee.
"He scarcely spoke as we were driving home.
He told me nothing of his jaunts in town.
I was afraid it wouldn't—*couldn't*—work,
this half and half arrangement."
Francis is badly shaken, more distressed
than Mrs. Bonner, though she too is sad.
"May be he saw Miss Lettice?" "Surely not!
He wouldn't know her." "But his mummer would."
"*You'd* better go to him. He may tell *you*."
Derrick has flung himself across his bed.
His sobbing checks when Mrs. Bonner comes.
He holds his breath and stiffens. A cold sponge
clapped to his back neck makes him gasp, then cry.
He lets his Bonner take him in her arms
and soother him as she did long ago.
"Tell Bonner what be wrong, then, and most like
she'll find a way to help. Now, don't you grieve
at them hard words to Delmer. Cherry knows,
and Francis, too, you didn't mean 'em, see?
Summat went wrong in London. Get it said.
—Did Derrick see Miss Lettice?" Derrick sobs.

He clings convulsively round Bonner's neck.
"I used to hate her. I don't hate her now.
I'd like to help her.
I threw a bottle at her. There's a scar
across her wrist. She wouldn't speak to us.
She said she wasn't Lettice. But she was.
I wrote to Mr. Hulbert. Then I wished
I never written. I'd forgotten her,
but when I saw her, I remembered then.
Mum knew her. But she just said 'My mistake'.
I wish I never wrote. She may be cross.
I told him what she calls herself. Oh, why,
why should she hide from him and use a name
that isn't hers? —Has she a bastard? Why,
oh, *why* do people get so hurt and sad?
Oh, why do bastards have to come at all?
—I never meant to tell you. I've done wrong."
"There, Derrick-boy, I don't believe it's so.
You may have done the very thing to help.
Come down and cuddle Delmer. Cherry too.
You'll feel yourself like, after. Then, may be,
you'll tell the hurt to Francis.
Be many riddles us can't reason out.
No need to let 'em daunt us."
('The child's full young to have it come so close,
the puzzle and the sorrow,' she reflects.)
He hugs his Bonner, wipes his tear-stained face,
then runs downstairs, jumping the last two steps.
He cuddles Delmer, who has ceased to cry,
kisses her mother, hangs on Conway's arm,
but shows he doesn't want to talk just now.
He's half asleep when Bonner comes with food.

He stirs, and when he sees the bowl is pleased.
He grabs his spoon, enjoys his bread-and-milk
down to the last drop, skilfully scooped up,
then settles into sleep with an eased sigh,
a child again, his adult gloom cast off.

* * * *

"*Good*-evening, Mr. Delmer! Pray step in.
My better-half will be indeed surprised,
delighted, too, yet more."
This is the first encounter of the men,
but Briggs has seen old photographs in Wilts.
"I'd like to speak to Mrs. Briggs alone
if it's convenient." "Why, surely, Sir!
No one shall interrupt. My weekly bills
demand my presence in the scullery
—my temporary office. *This* way, Sir.
Flora, my love, a visitor for you,
one unexpected, but as welcome, Sir,
as a warm day in winter."
Briggs trips away, wiping his sloppy lips
on a bright handkerchief, and sweating tact.
"You've guessed, perhaps, what I have come to ask?"
Flora's distressed embarrassment makes speech
too difficult to manage.
She pushes out a chair, but Hulbert stands.
"I've heard from Derrick." Flora reads, then gulps.
Hulbert's looks question her, compelling speech.
"We saw Miss Delmer, but she wished, it seemed,
to keep herself anonymous, and so
I thought it better to be reticent."
"*Did* she look ill?" "Well—I'm afraid she did."
"You have no clue to help me?" Flora twists

a corner of her handkerchief, and blinks.
"No clue at all?"
"Why, Sir, it grieves me. . . I can hardly dare
to say what crossed my mind. I may be wrong."
"I need your help, not pity. Get this out."
But pity—still—makes speaking difficult.
Words come at last, but slowly, with more gulps.
"Someone was with her. I don't know her name.
She used to visit at the hospital,
the Special hospital. . ." The voice tails off.
Hulbert compels his lips to utter words
he hates to utter.
"You mean my sister may have been with her
because she needed help? The sort of help
a Rescue Worker gives?" Silence assents.
"How can I trace her? What can you suggest?"
"She must have come from near.
Miss Delmer looked too weak to do much more
than cross the road. There's a big block of flats
just opposite—or was.
Suppose I go tomorrow, wait about,
and if I chance to see her, speak to her?
As like as not she'd put me in my place.
But if I said: 'Does Mara Stone need help,
because if so, her brother. . .'
she *might* persuade Miss Delmer to give leave.
She'd never tell without it. They just *can't*,
these Rescue Workers, Sir. . .
They've *got* to keep things private, or the girls
would never trust them."
Hulbert's thanks falter. From the past there comes
a plea for mercy, harshly put aside,

a hurtful mutter: 'whore', that scalds him now.
He presses Flora's hand, and blunders out.

*   *   *   *

Lettice is clad in a blue overall,
faded and dingy, patched in darker blue
on either elbow. Her thin legs are bare.
She rests her plimsolled feet against the pipes.
A baby's vest she's knitting for a friend
lies on her lap.
She stares before her at the bile-green wall,
tears coursing down her cheeks.
"What's up with Mara?" "What's the matter, duck?"
Doncher feel well, love?" "Try a peppermint."
"I've got some scent, dear." "Take a *big* sniff, duck."
"Oh, you're such dears; you *are* so kind to me.
It seems so rude—Please try to understand.
Try to forgive me."
"Don't you cry, Mara. Tell us what's amiss."
"We won't be crorss at anytink you say."
"It won't seem rude." "You go on. Speak your mind."
"It hurts when I'm so fond of you to hear
you use those nasty words and laugh so loud
at jokes that are so ugly.
We're all in the same boat here: I know that.
I *don't* forget it. Oh, forgive me, please!"
"*That's* all right, Mara." "We're not crorss wiv you."
"Them words, they don't mean nothing. They just
come."
"You mustn't let them fret you." "You cheer up!"
"You gotter larf at somefink in this place;
there ain't a lot to larf at."
"Let's have a sing-song. That'll do her good."

"Start Tipperary." "Mara, you begin."
"You sing so lovely, if you start us off
we'll hit the note first try."
"Let Mara sing first verse and us join in
and sing the chorus with her." "Yes, that's right."
Lettice blinks back her tears. She sings the verse
in a small voice, but tuneful. Then the girls
join in the chorus. Some of them sing flat,
but all sing bravely.

* * * *

Lettice has told the Matron who she is,
and asked her leave to have her brother come.
Matron has made few comments. Not for her
is moral censure; nor is she disposed
to utter exclamations based on zest
in contrast's relished melodrama—wheels
that come full circle, more like circus hoops
than as the chiaroscuro in a life
made tragic by the folly of the free.
She writes a pass for Hulbert. "Send him this."
('Admit the bearer to the parlour', signed
with neat initials.) "When I hear he's come
I'll send a nurse to fetch you. There's no need
for any speculation to arise."
"I'm grateful, Matron." Lettice turns to go,
her bearing meek as any Novice's
receiving orders on her clothing-day.

* * * *

From even the parlour walls pictures are banned
as unhygienic. The strait room, bricked off
from one much larger, is by far too high,
as ill-proportioned as a convent cell

in a converted mansion.
Lettice has come on noiseless plimsolled feet
and waits with folded hands: a nun-like form
that wards off kisses. Hulbert, too aghast
to greet his sister with articulate speech,
stands, eyes cast down in bitter misery.
He listens to the story that she tells:
her flight from Pagnell and her stay at Pyrte,
her love for Fennemore and his for her,
her arrogance, his frenzy, the event;
her own infection and her own despair;
her plunge to the scummed water.
                                        Her hands move;
they spread themselves, palms upward; her eyes lift.
"Then, Hulbert, something altered.
I prayed for Hugh's salvation as I sank.
And as I prayed—prayed in the Father's name—
I knew that when he hurtled through the air
he too had cried for mercy on his soul.
I saw no vision and I heard no voice;
I knew: how I can't say; I simply knew.
And when I sank the second time and prayed
for mercy in the Son's name, I was sure
that he in dying somehow had a share
in the strange Mystery of Christ's own death
—since he was penitent, since he was loved.
And when I sank the third time and cried out
for mercy in the Holy Spirit's name,
I felt quite sure he had been granted Life:
in Purgatory, torment: yes, but Life
in Paradise. I felt him safe; absolved.
My own salvation, or the lack of it,

I did not think of then. Later, I found
that though for Hugh I *could* pray—for I did—
I could not pray for mercy on *my* soul."
Again her hands are folded, her lids drooped.
"It seemed that if I died as I was then
—aware of sin, but not set free from sin—
I should not be with Hugh as I'd supposed,
suffering together with him: but alone.
That threefold plunge, willed in my cowardice,
seemed Satan's baptism—a mockery.
I could not share the Mysteries of Christ,
or if I shared at all could only share
the Mystery of His Death. *I* could not hope
to be with Him in glory, share with Him
the Mystery of His Rising. Not for me
the blessed hope, the sure and certain hope.
That I had forfeited. My arrogance,
and then my cowardice, had cancelled hope.
Yes, it was arrogance, it was not lust
that damned me in the Cliff Hotel that night.
I would not trust: was certain *I* knew best.
I knew our love was holy: would not see
that even holy love may need to wait
when sin has smirched it: need to wait, subdued,
until the word is spoken, the ban raised.
It was my arrogance that sent him out,
devoid of hope, without me.
God's mercy took him, for—I *know*—he prayed.
But *I* am not absolved.
I cannot turn to Cherry and her child;
I cannot run to Mrs. Bonner's arms:
not because pride forbids it, but because

it would exploit her goodness, be too soft
a way of consolation and relief.
I cannot turn to Derrick: he would see
the scar on my thin wrist. I saw his eyes
fix on it once. I saw the memory stir.
He is a child, but could not be a child
if he were forced to face *me* day by day.
No, I must live my life as best I can,
with you to help me—Helen Cordell too—
but no one from that house whose blessed peace
I dare not undermine. Why, to do *that*
would be more base than hack its solid walls
flat, with a pick, leaving a rubble waste
for weeds to root in! As to where I'll go
when I am cured (and I am nearly cured)
I do not know. But there will be some place.
And I shall still be Mara. Bitterness
will be the only flavour on my tongue:
not cynic bitterness—medicinal.
Someday, perhaps, a heart of flesh will beat
where now a heart of stone is all I have.
Someday I'll dare to kneel beside the grave
where we saw Rendell Delmer laid to rest,
and where I should have seen, but did not see,
sweet Lois Delmer laid to rest with him.
And if that day should come, I'll sign my name
as Lettice Delmer—happy one—once more.
Though was I ever happy? I think not."
The voice to Hulbert seems another voice
than his young sister's. He is pierced to hear
it speak of 'Rendell Delmer', pierced *more* deep
to hear it, sundered and unnatural,

speaking of 'Lois Delmer.' Mara Stone
seems to take on bitter reality.
He stands in silence. He can shield his eyes
so that they do not see the haggard face,
the plimsolled feet, the faded overall,
but he is forced to listen to the words
with which his sister dunts his grieving soul.
And now the porter raps. The hour has struck.
They do not kiss. Nor do their cold hands meet.
Mara's are folded on her narrow chest.
She goes in meekness, makes her way once more
to the girls' Common-room, picks up the vest
that she has finished knitting. She must thread
a silken ribbon at the neck and sleeves,
then wrap the vest in tissue, beg a box
from a good-natured nurse. All that she does
she does absorbed in what she has to do.
She knows no pity for her bare-legged self.

* * * *

Derrick has planned a dozen moves ahead.
Francis has failed to note the boy's intent
and gets his bishop jammed: has no defence.
Derrick sweeps boldly on and takes his rook.
He mutters: "Check", then sits back in his chair
while Francis ponders. "Yes, it's mate all right.
A very pretty piece of strategy!
Give me a knight next game."
Already Derrick's setting up the board.
Beside them Delmer prattles on her rug,
rattling the tin Derrick has filled with stones.
But Derrick barely hears. Nor is he roused
by the post falling through the letter-box.

Francis, for once, is more alert than he.
"You'd rather leave the letters till we've done?"
The youngster nods his head and takes a pawn.
Cherry comes running in. " 'Tis come!" she cries.
Francis tears open the tough envelope
and Derrick suddenly becomes aware
that Francis has been listening for the post.
He is annoyed; he flushes as he sweeps
the pieces from the board. "This game won't count.
I shouldn't really win it if you lost."
But Francis does not hear—or does not heed.
"He's won a major scholarship! Well done!"
"Oh, I be glad: and Mummer will be glad!
Oh, let me hug you, Derrick-boy! Why, look,
Delmer be holding out her arms. *She's* proud!"
The boy, cheeks crimsoned, suffers Cherry's hug;
then doubles down—nuzzling the child's cool neck
with his hot face, tickling her small soft sole—
to hide his deep embarrassment and joy.

* * * *

Hulbert for snail-paced years has toiled and grieved
in the Far East. The notes Lettice has sent
have told him almost nothing.
At last the Army frees him. He returns
to Chelsea and research. Lettice, he trusts,
will make her home with him, will leave the rooms
in Soho which she shares with the wronged girl
who once was fellow-patient, now is friend.
Lettice refuses, gently, gratefully,
but with such resolution that he sees
he will not move her.
Utterly baffled by his sister's choice

to live with someone quite unsuitable,
and work long hours in a job yet more
unsuitable—almost unmentionable,
he goes, distraught, to Helen.
"She will not draw her money from the bank,
because, she says, her name is Mara Stone,
not Lettice Delmer. It accumulates,
and meanwhile she subsists on what she earns
at that impossible job.
She needs to see a doctor—or a priest,
but when I urge it she just smiles at me,
and says: 'But, Hulbert, I'm not ill, am I?
And though I know I'm wicked, could a priest
make me less wicked'?" "I should let her be.
It must be hard. Oh, *hard*! Even *my* heart
is wrung. And yet—
she *may* be where she *should* be. . .
I don't believe she suffers through her job.
I think she drops in pennies, wipes the seats,
gives change when people need it, just as though
she was a tree stripped of its summer leaves,
left bare to winter—but with spring ahead.
She feels no sort of pity for herself.
There is no melodrama, no false pose,
no morbid immolation. She just feels
that Lettice Delmer's gone, and this strange job
is right for Mara Stone.
I found her singing last time I went down.
It was a song her mother wrote and set
to music. It was difficult, you know,
to find a job to suit her. We tried hard.
You see, she's trained for nothing, and she's frail.

She herself found this job—to our surprise.
She told us, smiling—not in irony—
but genuinely pleased to have found work
that wouldn't call for powers she hasn't got.
She may be getting odd, but would it help
to make her see a mental specialist?
If she can cope with life on life's own terms,
why shouldn't she?" "I would give both my hands
if I could see her in the Wiltshire house,
in Mrs. Bonner's care."
There is a ring from Helen's telephone
and Hulbert, with a sigh, gets up to go.
"Don't go. I've more to say. This won't take long.
My friends up north. A trunk call. We'd arranged—
Hullo! It's you. . . Yes, I will come for sure
—unless something prevents me. Oh, don't tease!"
Her bubbling laughter shows she is not hurt.
"Yes, *very* well: bursting with health. And you?
I'm glad. And Jessica's no worse? That's fine!
I've had a lovely birthday!
The daphne came this morning: violets too.
That Cornish nursery packed them beautifully.
Thee didn't ought to have 'em sent: them's dear."
Hulbert's aware of some small private joke.
"But I'm so glad you did! Tell Jessica
I sniff and sniff and take great breaths of spring.
The papers say you've frost up in the north:
make Jessica wrap up if she goes out.
—It's pipping. No, no more. Goodbye! I'll come."
Hulbert has sat averted and withdrawn,
and yet has sensed the ripple of delight
that ran through all the trivial colloquy.

And when she turns and comes to him again,
he notes her shining eyes, her springing gait.
She wears no ring; her only ornament
is an old brooch gay as a peacock's tail.
"I was about to say that I feel sure
she'll let you take her out now and again.
Don't try too hard to rouse her.
Take her by boat to Greenwich when it's warm.
Take her to see some pictures: quiet ones,
kind tranquil landscapes—Crome and Constable.
Talk of her mother if *she* talks of her.
I was relieved to hear her sing that song.
She sang so naturally, so tranquilly.
I shouldn't press the Wiltshire house. Someday
she may herself suggest you take her there.
But she can't be the Lettice you once knew,
or thought you knew.
You mustn't want to see *her* come again."
"Well—I won't harry her." He takes his leave,
a broken man, grizzled, with furrowed skin,
grieved and bewildered.

* * * *

Derrick has buried Delmer in the hay.
From her curl-tousled head he picks the stalks.
Francis and Cherry come with baskets packed
about their sleeping baby. Cherry's hands
are clasped by her twin daughters,
babbling a theme that Cherry understands,
though it is wordless. Francis shoves the pram,
and Mrs. Bonner follows with the milk.
Derrick prepares a tuffet of dry hay,
checking his godchild with a friendly frown

when she, with tugs and sallies, tries to romp.
"Delmer, m' duck, come sit ye quiet now.
Be time for picnic not for frolicking.
Derrick be hungry." Derrick proves this true.
He is as tall as Francis, and his voice,
no longer a child's treble, rules him out
from singing as a boy in the Church choir.
He serves instead, handing the bread and wine.
His sin in wounding Lettice is absolved,
along with other tantrums. He's a boy,
with boyish faults and failings, boyish whims,
but there is nothing morbid in him now;
he neither broods nor panics. Once a year
he spends a week with Flora. Briggs, in Leeds,
paying *his* annual visit, irks no more
than do his garish postcards, shoved aside
without a comment.
The picnic now is over. Delmer pouts
to see her hero snatch his sweater up,
signal 'I'm coming' to a schoolfellow
and lope away to join him for a bathe.
"Delmer, m' love, come feed them bobbing ducks?"
On Conway's shoulder Delmer pouts no more.
The twins, Cherry between them, babble still
and stagger on, each with a crust to throw.

*   *   *   *

Week after week, month after month plods on.
Hulbert takes pains to curb his misery
and follow Helen's counsel.
Mara's ways irk him, but he does not strive
to rouse her from her tranquil apathy.
They listen to his records: Handel, Bach,

or plainsong chants from Solesme. Now and then
they go to Evensong at Chelsea Church.
Each night but Sunday she is tied by Joan,
who shares her bed in Soho, seldom wakes,
but can't be left in *case* she waked and screamed.
"Let's see, how old is Joan now?" "She's just five.
She'll go to school in April. That'll help.
She needs more milk than Ireen can afford.
Ireen can't often get a chorus job,
and selling programmes is so poorly paid."
Hulbert has schooled himself to check the frown
that used to come when Lettice said Ireen.
"But, Hulbert, it would be unkind and rude
to say 'Irene'," Lettice said, dismayed,
when he protested. "Why, she *likes* her name!
To say 'It has three syllables in Greek'
—she'd think me crazed. What's Greek to
    Londoners?"
With Ireen and her daughter Mara finds,
and has found for five years, a peace of sorts.
The talk is not of music or of art,
but of the crocheted tray-cloths Ireen makes,
the vests that Mara knits,
Joan's dollies and Joan's ringlets and Joan's spots,
of whether it will rain or will be fine,
and where to find a shilling for the gas.
But there is kindness, there is courage too,
more restful in that each is unaware
that she is brave or kind. The two jog on;
neither is benefactress, neither asks
for thanks or praise; they have no scales to weigh
Mara's long sessions near the sleeping child

against the beans or kippers Ireen serves,
to time and piping hot, when Mara homes,
chilled by her ten hours sojourn underground.
Helen accepts the life of her loved friend
without rebellion. Hulbert can't accept,
but must endure, his quiet sister's choice.
He swallows down his misery and waits.

* * * *

A cistern slooshes water, then glug-glugs.
A heavy door is slammed. A penny drops.
Steps pass this way and that.
"And how's our Mara? Coo! I bet you're chilled!"
"Oh, not too bad. I've got my little stove."
"How you put up beats me. Airless *and* cold.
I'd die, I know I would."
"Oh, no, you wouldn't! Why, I walk to work.
That warms me up. And twice—some days three
times—
I brew a pot of tea. Look! Have a cup?"
"No thank you, dear. I'm late. —I don't need change:
for once I've got a penny."
The regulars stream through. Edie moves on
and Mrs. Jackson comes.
"Oh, ain't it cold? You must be perished, girl."
"The winter's nearly over. Any day
we'll feel a touch of spring. And how's the boy?"
"He's getting on. —And so must *I* get on!
You've got a penny for two ha'pennies?
—Ta, dear." "You wouldn't like a cup of tea?"
"No, girl, I mustn't stay." A stranger comes.
"What a vile day! I'm sure the slush will freeze."
"Wouldn't some hot tea help? I've got two cups."

"A cup of tea? I don't mind if I do.
You're lucky to be down here in the dry,
with a stove, too, and *tea*. . ."
Mara holds out the graceless stranger's cup,
and answers simply, not in irony:
"Yes, aren't I lucky? —Sugar? Help yourself."
The stranger takes two spoonfuls, heaped to spill,
and adds more milk. "A biscuit?" "Well, I grant
tea seems to *need* a biscuit." She takes three,
gobbles them down, accepts a second cup,
drinks, takes two pennies from her bulging purse,
slides them beneath her saucer, and goes off,
with a bare thank-you.
Mara's purse does not bulge. She adds the pence
to the few coins she has. She washes up,
then, since she is alone, she settles down
to knit and sing.

February Fill-dyke,
  Wash away the snow;
Leave no pie-bald patches
  Under the chill hedge-row

Where the north wind rivels
  Every shrinking thorn,
Shadowed by the cypress,
  Slighted by the sun.

Soon the birds will answer
  Fill-dyke's soft appeals:
Chirrup their halleluyas,
  Whistle their madrigals.

Footsteps approach: quick-tripping, skipping steps.
"I hoped I'd catch you in the morning lull.

I've been away. Up north. —Mara, my dear,
I'm to be married." "Helen! Oh, I'm *glad*!"
"I've known Jim for ten years. My friend—his wife—
she was my friend at school. Now, she has died.
She was an invalid, was nearly blind."
Helen breaks off, perplexed by Mara's stare.
"Ten years: three months. . . What is the difference
between a well-cooked plaice and well-cooked dab?
With decent reticence. . . Not false. Not false. . ."
Mara seems dreaming, unaware she speaks.
Helen, astonished, waits till she comes back
to where she is. She does not question her,
but haltingly takes up her tale again.
"Jessica, that's Jim's wife—" A stranger comes.
"Can you oblige? I've got no pennies left.
This weather's fatal to me. —Thank you, dear.
I'm truly grateful. Have a peppermint."
The stranger goes. "Mara, we *can't* talk here!
I'll come tonight while Ireen's at the Stoll."
Mara sits dreaming when her friend has gone.
But soon she knits again, and sings again.
Some rather heavy footsteps clump downstairs.
She checks her song, but not till Flora Briggs
has heard—and recognised—her voice, aghast.
She sweeps past Lettice, blindly. Mara Stone
on this encounter must be Mara Stone.
But Lettice drops her knitting to her lap,
breathing a little faster than she did.
When Flora Briggs emerges, eyes to front,
Lettice has risen. She has dropped her work
(and does not know it) on the slushy floor.
She steps towards Flora. "Mrs. Briggs, don't go.

I want to say I'm sorry."
Instinctive tidiness compelling acts
of which her conscious mind is unaware,
Flora picks up the vest and holds it out.
"You shouldn't be here. Oh, it's *not* the job
for you, Miss Stone!" "But, Mrs. Briggs, why not?
It's simple work, and I'm not over strong."
"No, you don't look it. Mistress. . . Oh, I'm *sad*!"
"Forget me, Mrs. Briggs." "I can't. I *can't*. . ."
Flora stands gulping. Then she speaks again.
"You wouldn't come and see us one fine day?
I hardly like to ask. . . But I'd be *proud*.
Here's our address. We have to have a card
for business purposes." "I'd *like* to come.
Thursday is my half day." "*Our* best day, too!"
A stranger comes, and Flora sighs and goes.
She feels a sudden need to hurry home
and tell her tale to Briggs.
She pours it out.
He croons astonishment and sympathy,
with many oohs and ahs, his fond goodwill
as patent as the blob of cottonwool
on his ill-shaven chin.

* * * *

When Hulbert visits Pagnell he brings gifts,
feeling them trifles, incommeasurable
with what the old house offers to its guests,
whether or not its guests are capable
of making theirs its proffered benison.
Derrick has never wholly lost his awe
of Hulbert, but each time a visit nears
he grows more eager for his company.

Hulbert brings offprints from the B.M.J.,
explains the technicalities, spurs on
the boy to question. Sometimes they go off
for whole-day walks together, Hulbert pleased,
even a little touched to be preferred
to Derrick's schoolmates. One day, coming back
from a long tramp, the conversation turns
on where Derrick will live when he goes up
to London as a student. They discuss
whether a hostel would be best or digs.
"Or I *could* live at Lambeth. —But I think
I'd rather see my mother once a week,
on Sunday evenings." Beaming, Mr. Briggs
goes off each Sunday after his bo-peep.
He takes his trombone, plays it in the Park
when it is fine, at Gospel Happy Hours;
and when it's wet he plays it in the hall
connected with his chapel.

* * * *

"Enter, Miss Stone: a very welcome guest
at our abode—humble, but yet, I trust,
hospitable as any Stately Home.
My better-half awaits you. Pray allow. . .
The superfluity of damp shall drip
within the kitchen sink. These days are sent,
I sometimes think, to test us. Tearful skies
should be a stimulus to cheerful thoughts."
Flora's perturbed to see her guest so wet.
"My slippers would seem army boots, but still. . . ?"
Mara Stone peels her sodden stockings off
and with her handkerchief attempts to dry
her cold wet toes. But Flora re-appears

with a warm towel. "You think of everything!
—Please call me Mara, would you, not Miss Stone?"
"Just which you like, dear." Flora rubs her feet,
"Stay where you are for tea. This skirt of mine
would take a pair of you, so don't you move
or it might tumble off." Briggs comes with tea.
Soon they are eating thickly buttered toast
around a blazing fire. Then Briggs bears off
the piled-up crocks, adroit; but soon returns.
"My queen, perhaps our guest would condescend
to turn the pages of our scrap-album
and view our snaps of Leeds and Leigh-on-Sea?"
He croons the question to his better-half
not to her visitor, in modesty.
The pleasure Mara shows is genuine.
She looks at every picture, nods her head
appreciatively as Mr. Briggs describes
the churches and the bridges and the parks
in an ebullient monologue of praise.
That Mr. Briggs has to avert his face
and coax his dentures back where they should be
(apologising with profuse regret)
clearly does not put off the visitor.
When every picture has been scanned and praised
he takes a ball of twine and deftly weaves
elaborate patterns on his fingertips,
and Mara begs him do them all again
more slowly so that she herself may learn
and show them off to Joan. She flushes up,
pleased when her aptitude receives its due
—indeed much more than is its due—of praise.
Cat's-cradle laid aside, Flora entreats

her guest to sing. She sings her mother's songs.
Briggs is enthralled. "Bravissima! Encore!"
But Mara has her eye on Flora's watch.
"You shan't be late. You're going to have a cab."
She sings again, while Flora fills a tin.
"Tomorrow's snack," she says, and sails away
to fetch the well-worn shoes and shiny skirt.
Briggs sidles off to don his mackintosh
and his galoshes. "Keep the stockings, *please.*
They'll warm your feet when you are underground."
"But, Flora. . . Oh, how generous you are!
And I'm afraid I'll have to ask a loan
to pay my cab-fare." "Oh, but not a *loan*!
Why, it's our little gift, if you'll accept. . ."
"I *will* accept! Oh, thank you *very* much.
It's been a lovely evening."
The women kiss, for Briggs is hovering.
"The chariot is here, love, at our door.
The rain is not excessive." "—Oh, my gamp!"
"I have it ready. I will shelter you,
then tell your Jehu whither he must wend.
You'll come again, Miss Stone?" "I'll love to come.
But call me Mara, please, and not Miss Stone."

* * * *

The post has come. Derrick has heard it drop.
The only letter is for him, he finds.
He opens it topspeed, and reads it once,
then, without pausing, hurries from the house.
He heads for the post-office. As he rides
he whistles Tar-ra-ra-de-boom-de-ay.
He grabs a form and writes: Thank you yes please.
He cycles home, still whistling.

He thrusts the letter into Conway's hand.

> Dear Derrick, runs the letter, probably
> you'll choose a student's hostel or else digs,
> but I've a bedroom—small—that you could have.
> I haven't any news, so Goodbye, Hulbert.

Conway's delighted; Mrs. Bonner too.
The boy might get a chill, or work too late. . .
She does not speak of Lettice. She reflects:
'Derrick be grown that steady, he'll not quail
to mark her wrist and think back to the time
when he was all at odds within himself.
Then he were jealous; now there be no call,
with him her mother's heir, and her so sad:
though sad not as she were, the Lord be thanked.'
Flora has been to Pagnell recently,
and talked of Mara.
"She's not stand-offish as she was that time
we went to see the mummies. Briggs and her,
they're thick as thieves. They played duets last night
on the harmonium. She doesn't seem
well—barmy. A bit childish. Thin, of course,
but not a scarecrow."

* * * *

Sunday is Derrick's Lambeth day. Poor Briggs
has bought a concertina: the trombone
drew protests from his colleagues. His wet mouth
made him uncertain as to time and tune.
He took the criticism very well,
and gave away the trombone. By the time
Derrick returns to Chelsea, Mara's gone.
They meet at last. Briggs has a swollen face

—which might be mumps.
The meeting brings no tension. Derrick's eyes
neither avoid nor seek the wrist that's scarred.
The swollen face *is* mumps. The next two weeks
Mara finds Derrick looking out for her.
When Briggs is well he has to go to Leeds,
and Flora with him. Vi has had a turn,
lingered a week or two, and then passed on.
Hulbert is glad that Derrick stays at home:
he has a stuffy cold. Derrick can see
that he is drowsy and will be relieved
to have his quiet sister kept amused.
He murmurs nonsense in the furry ear
of Sooty's grandson, brought from Foursquare House,
and Lettice smiles. Hulbert's thoughts flash ahead.
He has a sudden vision of the boy
grown to a man, caressing on his knee
a child as wanton as the youthful cat.
The vision pleases Hulbert. Lonely age
—for he himself will never, that he knows,
be bonded to a wife—he can accept,
Derrick must woo and marry, make a home
solid as Foursquare House. He drowses off,
leaving the boy and woman to achieve
friendly security through jest and chat.
Lettice responds to Derrick's every lead,
now by a word, now by a wordless smile.
They go to Evensong, and then combine
in making bread-and-milk and scrambling eggs.
Lettice announces almost casually:
"I've given in my notice." "At your job?
You *have*!" Hulbert exclaims. "That's famous news!"

"And I'll be leaving Soho before long.
Perhaps I'll find a residential post.
I'm so much plumper."
"Though you are plumper, you're not all that plump,"
Hulbert observes. "You'll need a holiday."
"Why not go down to Pagnell," Derrick cries.
"I'm going for a week-end fairly soon.
We could go down together." "Yes, I'll come,
if Cherry will allow me." "Why, of course!
They will all love to have you. Always—still—
they call the room you used to have your room.
There's a hair-tidy I made years ago. . .
Do write and say you're coming." "Lettice, do."
Hulbert is grateful: had the plea been his
he knows it must have lacked simplicity
and candour. In it the harsh-visaged past
would have grimaced. It would have husked his
    voice.
"I must go north before I go to Pagnell."
"Go north? —But where?" "A place called
    Bittersby.
I can't explain. I may when I come back."
"Just as you like, of course." Hulbert's amazed
at the new self Lettice has just revealed
so undramatically, so evenly;
but his amazement is not half so great
as his relief and joy. He sits and stares
into the fire when he is left alone
while Derrick is escorting Lettice back
to Joan and Ireen. Quiet comes to him
as quiet comes to mountains after storm,
the rumbling thunder silenced, and the dusk

turning to folded gauze boulders and scree.

*   *   *   *

Lettice has travelled through the night, alone.
Her destination is a Rectory
approached by lane and field-path. The sky's blue,
with scuds of cloud that threaten. She is calm,
although aware of an ordeal ahead
too fierce for human strength.
Knowing her body's frailty, she waits,
leaning against a tree, in the bright sun,
strengthened by hazel-catkins and the song
of blackbirds and of thrushes, and the sense
of all the spring-tide promise in the wood.
After her rest she walks on steadily.
She need not hurry; it is early still;
she does not wish to be before the time
of her appointment.
The field-path joins the high road; straight ahead
she sees her destination gaunt and vast,
built of the same grey stone as the grey Church,
its garden and the churchyard side by side,
their flimsy railing, rusted, lying prone
and almost hidden by the encroaching weeds.
The headstones that tell the passers-by whose graves
they see,
crumbling and askew,
are clumsy and ill-designed, their lettering uncomely.
Lettice stares at one, newer than the others
but stained blotchily where a fungus sullies it.
Its chiselled truth, though it startles and horrifies her,
yet strikes her as inexorably destined,
ineluctable as an eclipse.

In memory of Rachel Fennemore,
beloved wife of Richard Fennemore. . .
Lamentation and weeping, and great mourning:
Rachel, weeping for her child,
would not be comforted. . .

Storm clouds shroud the sun,
grey as the memorials
that top the ragwort and the uncropped dead-nettles.
The promise of the morning yields rudely
to hail.
The squall, as though malevolent,
hurtles its catapultings.
Tremulous and cowering under its assaulting,
Lettice Delmer shrinks,
flayed by a sense that each unkindly missile
wings at her solely,
aimed with vile precision,
by a demon or a harpy.
She covers her face helplessly,
visited by a fear that is not a physical fear.
She is meeting some menace hostile as hell's menace,
an onslaught not nature's but, rather, old Satan's,
(old as the universe)
that hard-bit, slick-tongued, hideously subtle old
    Satan,
who once before, years ago, with vile cunning stealth,
had schemed direfully to possess his cringing victim.
Onslaught such as Hugh knew likewise
out on the cliff at Brixwell,
racked by terror, by despair, driven frantic by
    remorse,
dumbfounded and alone, until he dived.

The Devil's darts, age-old yet brand-new missiles,
poised to stab,
like some malign weasel-fly's,
seem assured of triumph in an easy victory.
But Lettice, hands before her face to ward off
the hail,
stumbling and blundering across the graveyard,
her knees almost too weak to bear her,
hardly aware of her confused intent to reach the
Church for shelter,
suddenly knows again the certainty
that Hugh's remorse (as he hurtled seaward)
changed blessedly to penitence,
knows his Eleison found answer,
knows the strong man armed met a Man stronger,
knows Hugh safe,
knows his purgation certain,
and, knowing this, pushes the heavy door,
stumbles blindly into the dark edifice,
heedless of mustiness, heedless of grime and
cobwebs,
and sinks upon her knees.
After a while she rises,
leaves the dank Church, crosses the graveyard,
and tries to ring the rusted bell by the blistered and
peeling Rectory door.
It gives no ring, only creaks emptily.
She batters the door with whitened knuckles.
Hugh's father opens it.
She sees Hugh's eyes, Hugh's forehead,
but the hair is thin and soiled,
the face withered, its lines limned by misery.

"Why have you come?" "You said 'Come'." "Ever since
I've wished I had said 'Don't'."
"Let me come in." "Come in, then, if you must.
We are both fools to face this interview.
The past is dead. Not buried. And it stinks."
"I saw the stone—the headstone. Ah, I'd thought
to find Hugh's mother—."
"Sit down if you can find a place to sit."
The words seem barked not spoken.
The chairs are littered with a mess of things:
a dirty cup and plate, unmended socks,
a cassock full of moth, and brown with age,
an album of old photographs, a cat,
mangy and very aged but not thin,
unopened letters with a bishop's seal.
Lettice sits huddled on a ruptured stool.
Now, in a different voice, hoarse and constrained,
Hugh's father speaks again. "Within an hour
of hearing of his death, she guttered out
like a blown candle."
Lettice's hands spring up to hide her face.
At last she looks at Fennemore and says
in a low voice that trembles:
"I'm certain he was penitent—forgiven."
"How are you certain?" Richard Fennemore
mutters the question almost with a snarl,
and Lettice flinches. "That I do *not* know.
But I *am* certain. Knowledge came to me
when I prayed for him, as I tried to drown.
I sank three times. I prayed three times. Three times. . .

And Father, Son, and Spirit heard my prayer.
My own forgiveness
I have not dared to ask—until today.
You are a priest. I beg of you to come
into your Church and hear me own my guilt.
If you can, then absolve me; if you think
I have not owned all my gross wickedness
then I must go on bearing sin, unshriven,
till God has worn away my heart of stone
and given me a humbler heart—of flesh.
Will you do this?" Hugh's father stares at her.
"How *can* I hear you? Girl—I haven't prayed,
but from a heart of—steel, since my boy sinned.
I've tried to stab at God as, when he sinned,
I stabbed at Hugh: at Rachel's child. . . Look
round—"
He makes a sudden gesture of despair.
"Is this the study of a priest of God?
Look at the grime. It is a sinner's room,
grimed with unfaith."
Lettice sits bowed. Still bowed, she says at last:
"But I have heard that when a priest has shriven
a humbled penitent, he adds the plea:
'And pray for me, a sinner'." "That is so."
The mumbled words are barely audible.
"I ask you, a third time, to hear my sin.
If I do wrong in asking—God forgive.
I have no strong conviction any more
that when I seem obedient to God's will,
I am obedient." Fennemore, convulsed,
stands silent. His clenched hands, their nails
untrimmed,

are bloodied by their clench.
At last he whispers. "Since I'm not *convinced*
that you do wrong, I'll come. It's *possible*
that God can use even me—" he hesitates,
"as mouthpiece for his mercy." Then he groans,
and, as he groans, he turns away, convulsed
even more sorely, more disturbingly.
"Leave me alone. Go to a worthier priest.
Why come to me? You are a lunatic
to come to me." With cold hands Lettice hides
her face. At last she stirs. Her voice is low
but it is steady, and she does not flinch.
"Give me the name, then, of another priest.
But send me off even without that help
if I am asking help I should not ask."
Now she stands up. But as she stands she sways;
she almost falls. "You need some nourishment.
Sit down again. I'll brew a pot of tea.
All that there is to eat is bread and cheese."
He clears a chair of litter.
"It will be better than that backless stool."
His voice is harsh although his words are kind.
Lettice sinks, helpless, into the deep chair.
She does not try to speak till she has drunk.
Then, rising, she puts out a trembling hand,
looks at Hugh's father through a blur of grief,
and stammers: "I had hoped you'd let me come
to work for you: to do what I could do
in house and church. But that's too much to ask,
so I must go." She moves towards the door.
"You could not do it." Fennemore's teeth grit.
"I am beyond *wanting* the church put right.

The chancel—bats have fouled it. No one comes:
except the dead, and those that bring the dead."
"I'd like to come." "You'd *like* to come? You're mad."
He eyes her blankly. Then he shrinks from her.
"If I should change my mind—why, then, I'd write.
I shall not write unless I change my mind."
Lettice holds out both hands.
"Ah, if you can, —forgive me. . . Oh, I know
it is a bitter thing, too much, to ask."
Tears brim and fall. Hugh's father blunders off,
drums with his fingers on the windowsill,
then turns and mutters: "Child, I'll hear your sins."
He drags his jacket from him, and pulls on
the rusty cassock and an old cloth cap
with a torn lining.

* * * *

When Lettice, shriven, passes from the nave,
Fennemore, huddled at the worm-bored chair
on which he sat to hear her, does not move.
She shuts the studded door as quietly
as its great weight allows, then makes her way
across the graveyard. She accepts as fact
divine forgiveness for her arrogance,
but though she's humbly thankful, she is not
exultant. Neither had she thought to be.
She did not come to seek the sudden bliss,
the surging joy, some penitents may find.
What she might feel to find herself absolved
was something that she did not think about
—and does not think about. Though she's forgiven,
the gravestone that she passes does not lie:
the dereliction at the Rectory

is dereliction still.
Her soul, though loosened from the fowler's net,
does not soar up ecstatic, like a lark
seeking the empyrean, rather halts
like some small sparrow fallen from its nest
—though not without its Father.
Lettice has never heard, nor Mara Stone,
the Risen Master speak her name at dawn,
nor does she hear Him now. She knows no urge
to cry 'Rabboni!' as she struggles on.
The prayer within her heart and on her lips
forms in response to the deep anguished cry
that broke on her from Richard Fennemore,
as, shriven, she rose up, raddled with tears,
to say her penance in the frass-soiled nave.
She prays for him, a sinner, as she prayed,
three times, when she was drowning, for his son.
"Eleison! Eleison!" she prays,
and then again "Eleison!", intent
on him for whom she prays and on his need.
The prayer demands all her vitality:
it leaves no surplus that can overflow
in pæans and ecstasy.
Nor when she reaches London and takes up
the common threads of daily life again
does any sudden glory shine on her
reflected from the Light of lights above.
She moves in neutral twilight like one lost
who, before dawn, treads softly,
thankful that blackness merges into grey
rather than hopeful of a roseate east.
She goes about her business soberly:

tackles a pile of mending for Ireen;
lets Derrick take her out to Kew one day;
confides in Hulbert in a calm long talk
one Sunday evening in his Chelsea rooms
while Derrick is at Lambeth.
He still goes
at times when Briggs is likely to be out,
is still embarrassed when Briggs bows and smirks
and shows ebullient amity. Today
he steels himself to meet Miss Emmy Briggs,
who up till now has kept herself aloof,
unable to face strangers.
He is relieved to find Flora alone.
Emmy has gone with Briggs, to give out tracts.
"She's plucky, poor old girl, but it's hard work
to stick old Flora when you want your Vi.
Nat does his level best to fill the gap
but he can't bicker. Bickering's meat and drink
to poor old Em, and so it was to Vi.
I've grown too fat and lazy. —Listen, love,
next Sunday's Chestnut Sunday. Bushey Park?
Better than staying put like two old hens
shut in a coop all evening?" "Sorry, no.
I'm going down to Pagnell." "So you are!
And Mara's going with you.
Tell her she needn't bother packing lunch.
I'll send Nat round with sausage-rolls—and books:
a *Lady* and a *Tatler* and a *Queen*."
"Get him to take them round to Soho, Mum.
We shall be out. We're going to celebrate."
"Celebrate what?" "Oh, just a prize I've won."
"You never said. . . Why, what a clam you are!

You'll take out the King's gall-stones some fine day
and never tell your Mum. —*We*'ll celebrate
when you get back. Would Mara come along?"
"She might stop on at Pagnell. Or perhaps
she will have found a job where she'll live in
—one not in London." "But she needs a rest.
She pitched a dummy going back last week.
Nathaniel had to chase a cab, poor lamb,
and leave her propped against a pillarbox."
A wonder flits that has not come till now.
"What do you call her, son?" "Just 'you' — or 'her'.
At Pagnell she'll be Lettice."
"There'll be another kid in a few days,
so Mara told me." "Yes, they're pleased at that."
"Let's hope this time as it will be a boy."
Voices are heard and Flora stretches out
to set a waiting saucepan on the stove.
"Now you'll be introduced to Emmy, son."
Briggs hurries forward with his hand stretched out.
"Ah ha! Ah ha! The prize-winner's still here.
Bravo! Bravo!" "You'll introduce me, please."
Emmy is huffed; she seems to hiss the words.
Briggs seeks to compensate for his *faux pas*
by drumming on his breast with both his hands.
"For*give* me, sister. —Mr. Tort: Miss Briggs."
" 'Aunt Emmy' I had thought. But I suppose
I'm too low-class for prize-winning young men."
Derrick, confused, mutters: "Now, how on earth—"
"*Nat* read it in the *paper*. I was *shocked*
to see my *brother* read a *news*paper
on *Sun*day, in the *Park*." Briggs wrings his hands.
"The man who plays the trombone—oh dear, dear!

It was beneath my eyes before I knew. . ."
"An opportunity to witness—lost."
'An angry goose might shut its beak just so,'
Derrick reflects, avoiding Flora's eye.
"You'll have some cocoa, Emmy, and a bun?"
"My queen, we'll *all* have cocoa."
Derrick, refusing cocoa, shakes once more
Miss Emmy's coldly proffered fingertips,
and—which he does not often do—holds out
a friendly hand towards Briggs.
To see Briggs bullied when he is so kind
makes him endure the over-eager grasp
and clammy palm with equanimity.
Briggs sees him to the door, a grateful man,
and bows him out as though he were a prince.

* * * *

Hulbert treads lightly when he leaves Soho.
He feels no dread that Lettice will evade
the Pagnell visit. She has bought herself
stout hobnail brogues. For these, and chocolates
for Cherry's children, she has paid in cash.
The last of Mara's savings will be spent
tomorrow when she pays her railway fare;
but she has packed her cheque-book. She demurred
when Hulbert said that he would see her off.
He acquiesced, thinking the past might rise
too vividly, perhaps, if he were there.
Derrick will go straight from the hospital,
cutting a lecture to be there in time.
Although no word has come from Fennemore,
Lettice is equable. She still may hear;
and if she does not—well, it will not mean

that all is hopeless. *She* may not be used
to clear the grime and misery away,
and yet it may be cleared—since he has prayed
and she has prayed. All this her brother knows:
some she has told him, some needs not be told.

* * * *

The ducks are being fed; they quack and squawk,
Francis is mowing the fresh-smelling lawn.
The rooms are ready: aired and gay with flowers.
Derrick is still a hero to the girls.
They're all excited. It's half term today
at Pagnell High School: Delmer's free to help.
The little ones go to the village school;
they like it, but today they're envious:
they'd wanted to help Granmer.
Derrick has talked of Lettice. Martha too,
though never very clever with her tongue,
has made them long to see her.
"This used to be her home," their granmer says.
"We've hopes as it may be her home again."
They wash their faces, let their curls be brushed,
put on clean frocks—as gay as butterflies;
then run to kiss their mother. Cherry's joy
has a profundity they cannot plumb,
but Francis plumbs—and shares—it.

* * * *

Helen, at breakfast, hears her telephone.
'Derrick, perhaps,' she thinks. 'He may have found
he can't cut that last lecture after all.'

She makes a rapid survey of her plans,
prepared, in need, to go to Paddington.
Not Derrick's voice, but Ireen's, choked and
hoarse. . .
"Oh come at once, Miss Cordell! Straightaway.
I'm that upset. It's *Mara*. Oh, she's *died*:
just now, and no one with her only Joan."
Then, in response to Helen's stammered gasp.
"*Doctor*? I never thought to ring-up *her*."
"Get Joanie off to school." Helen rings off.
She tells the doctor—who shows no surprise—
then hurries to Soho. She coaxes Joan
to eat a sandwich: left by Mr. Briggs,
with *Queens* and *Tatlers*. Ireen wrings her hands
and sobs: "To think that *she* will never turn
them pages, taste that tongue. . ."
Helen has buttoned on Joan's mackintosh.
She stuffs Joan's satchel up with sausage-rolls
to share at school in playtime.
Not crying now, Joan joins a schoolfellow
who calls her from the street, and Helen turns
towards the bedroom. "How you *dare*. . ." Ireen
can only sob and shudder.
Lettice lies
just as she lay in dying. Helen sinks
upon her knees beside her. No words form
in her hushed mind. (Later, she gropes for words
—when she is telling Hulbert—and they come
with profound swift conviction, so profound
and so intense that Hulbert's gladdened heart
misses a beat.

"Startled into Eternity by joy:
startled, yet peaceful—that is how she looked.")
Aware at last that Dr. Steele has come,
Helen goes out to join her in the hall.
"I can't get sense from Ireen." Ireen bolts,
with sobs, into the kitchen.
"*You'd* better talk to her and get the facts
—if you *can* get facts from her—while I look.
No need to have an inquest. With that heart—"
Ireen responds to Helen, but in jerks,
with many pauses, many sniffs and gulps.
"Joan says they both woke early. Mara sang
and, after, played cat's-cradle. Then she said:
'Give me a pencil, Joanie.' But the child
she couldn't find no pencil, so she give
some chalks out of her playbox.
Mara, she'd gone quite barmy, the poor girl.
She wrote: 'I leave the money in my bank
to Cherry's daughter, Delmer."
A kind of will she must have thought it was.
She wouldn't have no money in no bank;
what's more, she never signed it, for she put
not Mara Stone but—*Lettuce Delmer*. . . Queer!
Might have got muddled with the other name
as she'd just wrote? Why think of *lettuce*, though?
It seems a funny sort of *name*. Flowers make
such pretty names for girls." Ireen stops short.
She takes a drink of water at the sink,
and then, when Helen prompts, she speaks again.
"Soon, when she'd finished chalking—not her name
but what she thought her name was,
she give a loud cry, Joanie said, and stared

as if she saw someone she liked to see.
But what she cried was silly."
Ireen moves blindly to the mantelpiece.
"Don't think me heartless if I smoke," she gasps.
Miss Cordell strikes a match and holds it lit;
not till Ireen is smoking does she ask:
"What was the cry?" Ireen is loath to tell.
"Why, people's dying words—it's nice when they
say something, well—regelious." "Tell me though."
Ireen is still reluctant. When she speaks,
it is as though ashamed. Her voice is low,
her eyes downcast. "She called out: 'A bone eye.'
It doesn't make no sense. Eyes can't be bone."

* * * *

Derrick is in good time. He puts two bags
to book two seats. He watches, with bright eyes.
When Helen nears he grasps calamity
before she speaks. The two with one accord
go straight to Soho. On their way he hears
how death has come to Lettice.
Helen was not bewildered by the cry
misheard by Joanie; Derrick from a child
has known the story of the Tomb at dawn.
He listens without comment, holding back
the tears that threaten.
Ireen is at her window in Soho
watching for Helen. When they reach the flat
they find her waiting at the open door.
"A nurse has been, Miss Cordell: and you gone. . .
Oh dear, it did upset me. . . She's done now.
And Mara's brother's come. He went in *there*."
She jerks her thumb, and whispers.

"I give that paper to him what she chalked.
And, oh Miss Cordell, look! This letter's come.
The postmark's Bittersby, and Mara said:
'If one should come from Bittersby, be sure
to post it on at once.' And now, oh dear,
she's gone where letters can't be forwarded. . ."
Ireen alone can ease her pressured woe
by turning verbal taps. When Hulbert comes
he struggles to find earthly words to express
what is ineffable, and knows defeat;
as Helen does, and Derrick. The three stand
bonded but wordless by the open door;
then Hulbert beckons Derrick to approach
his quiet sister. Thought in each is hushed
by something more empyreal than thought.
At last thought stirs: the same thought in all three,
shared but unvoiced.
'Lettice she would have been, peace would have
    found,
in Foursquare House this evening.
But sempiternal peace, but purer joy,
for Lettice—'happy one'—greeted at dawn. . .'
At length speech comes, but comes with simple words
expressive not of deep and holy things
but of the need for action. "Let's go home.
We must write letters, Derrick." "*This* has come."
Hulbert receives the letter Helen hands,
and notes the postmark. "Bittersby. . ." He knows
the letter is from Richard Fennemore.
"It will be better if *you* write," he says,
and hands it back to Helen. "As you wish.
No need to read it. It would not have come

unless he'd changed his mind." Hulbert assents.
His eyes and Helen's meet—compassionate,
their thoughts unspoken.

* * * *

Francis and Delmer and her grandmother
wait for the train from London. Porter Bill
is Porter Bill no longer—he's too old—
but he has hobbled from his daughter's house
to pay his last respects.
Cherry is with her new-born son at home.
Old Martha weeps with her. The train draws up.
In Helen's hand there is a home-made cross
from Bittersby, relics of garden flowers
unconquered by the weeds: rue and sweet-brier,

> In memory of Lettice and of Hugh,
> from Richard Fennemore. Out of the deep. . .
> If Thou, O Lord, wilt be extreme to mark. . .
> Mercy with Thee, and plenteous redemption.

The mourners drive in silence through the lanes
hearing the bell toll nearer.
They reach the lych-gate. From the time-worn porch
the priest advances. Turning, he intones:

> I am the Resurrection and the Life.
> Remember not the sins. . . Let not your heart
> be troubled. In my Father's house. . .

Above the Delmers' grave a lark flings out
a pæan in ecstasy and innocence.

PLOT SUMMARY

****

Page 5: Lois Delmer, wife of Rendell Delmer, a Harley Street doctor, visits patients at a Special Hospital. Here, in the April of (we can presume) 1912, she meets Flora Tort, whom her husband has suggested as someone who might be helped by coming to live with them as a maid; they are also to help trace her little boy, and bring him to live with them. ***Page 17***: Mrs Delmer returns home to Highgate, to 3 Fitzroy Park, where her daughter Lettice, who is perhaps eighteen years old, is playing tennis with her half-brother Hulbert (Mrs Delmer's step-son, thirteen years older than Lettice) and a Highgate neighbour, Francis Conway. Some time later Flora and five year-old Derrick arrive; the arrangement is not a success. ***Page 37***: Dr Delmer, who has a weak heart, is to retire and live in Wiltshire, in Foursquare House in Pagnell Parva. He asks Flora to go too. But in August she, and her son, are revealed as thieves. Derrick hurls a bottle at Lettice, cutting her wrist. As he runs away Mrs Bonner, who does the family laundry at her cottage in Gospel Oak, arrives with her daughter Cherry. At the same time Hulbert and Francis Conway come home from lunching in town: Francis and Cherry meet. It is decided that Derrick should live with Mrs Bonner at Gospel Oak. Flora

****

goes away. ***Page 50***: Two years have passed, and the Delmer family are living in Wiltshire; the First World War has broken out. Cherry is now the Delmers' maid, but has been home for her two weeks' holiday. When she returns Lettice leaves for London and, *en route* to the Conways' house in Fitzroy Park, goes with Hulbert to call at Mrs Bonner's at Gospel Oak. A photograph reveals to Lettice that Francis Conway, with whom she considered that she had an understanding, is in love with Cherry. When she gets home she lies to her mother, telling her that Francis had proposed but that she refused him. ***Page 65***: Dr Delmer dies and Mrs Delmer has a stroke. Cherry looks after her devotedly; Lettice becomes more and more bored, lonely and bitter. Hulbert asks her to come and live with him in Chelsea, to paint and write. She goes to London, but because Hulbert is posted to France, moves in to a woman's hostel. Meanwhile, in Wiltshire, a contented *ménage* consists of Francis and Cherry, in a flat in the top of the house, and Derrick, Mrs Bonner and Mrs Delmer. ***Page 72***: Hulbert suggests that his sister go to a concert with a man he knew at Harrow. Lettice, inexperienced and naive, is assaulted by him. She is distraught, but resolves to get a job in an orphanage. Some weeks later Hulbert, on leave from France, is told by Lettice that she is pregnant; he does as she asks and recommends a doctor to terminate the pregnancy. She is utterly broken. ***Page 90***: Francis, who has been wounded at the Front, gets a job at Pagnell Grammar School; Derrick is godfather to his and Cherry's daughter, Delmer. A letter comes from Lettice saying that she is coming to Wiltshire. The family make excited preparations. However, at the station before Pagnell, called

****

Pyrte, something impells her to get off the train. The family at Foursquare House learn to their dismay that she is not coming. Lettice obtains work at a guest-house. ***Page 108:*** She falls in love with Hugh Fennemore, who is living at the guest-house because he has been ostracised by his family after having caught venereal disease. Meanwhile, Mrs Delmer has died, leaving the house to the Conways. Flora Tort writes to announce that she is now Flora Briggs and wants her son back. A kindly lawyer negotiates an arrangement whereby Derrick stays with the Conways but sees the Briggs's from time to time. ***Page 120***: Lettice, convinced that she and Hugh are as one, persuades him to sleep with her; she cannot understand his guilt and shame. He tries to persuade her that they should not see each other for three months. She, convinced of the truth of her own feelings, will not countenance this. They spend a night together. In the morning Hugh leaves Lettice sleeping. He drowns himself. She hears his death being discussed in the train back to London. It is November 1918. ***Page 136***: Using the name Mara Stone, Lettice is admitted to the Special Hospital as a venereal disease patient. Just before Christmas she tries to drown herself in the Thames. Helen Cordell (who has been visiting the Special Hospital for many years) rescues her and takes her back to her flat in a mansion block opposite the British Museum. Flora and Derrick, on a visit to the museum with Mr Briggs, see her. Helen realises that Mara Stone is Mrs Delmer's daughter. ***Page 149***: Back in Wiltshire, Derrick, deeply upset, tells Mrs Bonner that he had seen Lettice in London. Hulbert visits Flora to try and find out anything he can. Lettice goes back to the Hospital, apparently persuaded there by Helen. Hulbert visits her; she reveals to him the depth of her humiliation and despair. ***Page 158***: Derrick wins a scholarship to the grammar school. Hulbert goes to the Far East to work. After five years, in perhaps 1924, he returns to Chelsea, hoping Lettice will live with him. She refuses, preferring to stay with Irene, and her little girl Joan, whom she met in the hospital, and to go on working at her job as a public lavatory attendant. One day Flora Briggs comes there; it is Lettice who begs forgiveness. ***Page 172***: Derrick, now eighteen, goes to London as a medical student; he will lodge in Hulbert's flat in Chelsea. Lettice announces that she is leaving her job. She goes north to see Hugh's father at the Rectory, hoping to be reconciled with him. Derrick is to go with her to Wiltshire for the weekend. But on the morning of their departure it is discovered that her weak and overstrained heart has killed her. Her last words are 'Rabboni' (or 'Master', Mary Magdalene's cry of recognition when the resurrected Jesus appeared to her).